W9-BBE-027

ROOSEVELT BANKS
and the Attic of Doom

ROOSEVELT BANKS
and the Attic of Doom

Laurie Calkhoven

with illustrations by Debbie Palen

Clifton Park - Halfmoon Public Library

475 M

Clifton Park, NY 12065

ONE ELM BOOKS

Egremont, Massachusetts

One Elm Books is an imprint of Red Chair Press LLC

Red Chair Press LLC   PO Box 333   South Egremont, MA 01258-0333

www.redchairpress.com

Free Discussion Guide available online.

Publisher's Cataloging-In-Publication Data

Names: Calkhoven, Laurie, author. | Palen, Debbie, illustrator. | Calkhoven, Laurie. Roosevelt Banks.

Title: Roosevelt Banks and the attic of doom / Laurie Calkhoven ; with illustrations by Debbie Palen.

Description: Egremont, Massachusetts : One Elm Books, an imprint of Red Chair Press LLC, [2022] | Sequel to Roosevelt Banks : Good-Kid-In-Training. | Interest age level: 008-012. | Summary: "With a new sister on the way, Roosevelt Banks has to give up his bedroom and move into the attic, which must be haunted because of all the squeaks and groans coming from the spooky place at the top of the stairs. After his plan to move into a fort in the woods fails, and a ghost-busting exercise goes terribly wrong, Roosevelt—with the help of Tommy, Josh, and Eddie Spaghetti—has to find the courage to defeat the biggest, spookiest ghouls ever and turn the Attic of Doom into a Room with a View"--Provided by publisher.

Identifiers: ISBN 9781947159709 (hardcover) | ISBN 9781947159716 (ebook PDF) | ISBN 9781947159723 (ePub3-R S/L) | ISBN 9781947159730 (ePub3-R TR) | ISBN 9781947159747 (mobi TR)

Subjects: LCSH: Bedrooms--Juvenile fiction. | Attics--Juvenile fiction. | Haunted places--Juvenile fiction. | Courage--Juvenile fiction. | Friendship--Juvenile fiction. | CYAC: Bedrooms--Fiction. | Attics--Fiction. | Haunted places--Fiction. | Courage--Fiction. | Friendship--Fiction.

Classification: LCC PZ7.C12878 Roa 2022 (print) | LCC PZ7.C12878 (ebook) | DDC [Fic]--dc23

LC record available at https://lccn.loc.gov/2021937250

This book is a work of fiction. Any references to historical events, real people or real places are used fictitiously. Other names, characters, places, and events are products of the author's imagination, and any resemblance to actual events, places, or persons, living or dead is entirely coincidental.

Main body text set in 17/24 Baskerville

Text copyright © 2022 by Laurie Calkhoven

Copyright © 2022 Red Chair Press LLC

RED CHAIR PRESS, ONE ELM Books logo, and green leaf colophon are registered trademarks of Red Chair Press LLC.

All rights reserved. No part of this book may be reproduced, stored in an information or retrieval system, or transmitted in any form by any means, electronic, mechanical including photocopying, recording, or otherwise without the prior written permission from the Publisher. For permissions, contact info@redchairpress.com

Printed and bound in Canada

1121 1P FRNS22

For Isaac, a super cool dude.

CHAPTER ONE
The Summer of Dad

It was going to be the best summer ever. THE SUMMER OF DAD.

I jumped off the school bus yelling to the driver "Bye, Mrs. Angela! Have a good vacation." My three best friends, Tommy, Josh, and Eddie Spaghetti, were right behind me with a chorus of goodbyes.

"Bye, boys," Mrs. Angela called after us. "Don't get into too much trouble."

"Who, us?" I asked with an innocent grin. "What kind of trouble would good kids like us get into?"

Eddie Spaghetti snickered behind me. His name's not really Spaghetti, but once in second grade he laughed so hard at lunch that a spaghetti noodle shot out of his nose. It was the most awesome thing ever.

Mrs. Angela shook her head as the door wheezed shut and she drove off.

The smell of fresh cut grass tickled my nose. It smelled like summer. And fun.

"The last day of school for almost three whole months!" Josh said. "Did you hear how loudly I clapped? They could hear me all over the building!"

Every year on the last day of school we lined up and clapped while the fifth-graders walked the halls one last time. I guess we were supposed to be proud of them for getting promoted or some junk like that.

"Next year *we're* going to be the fifth-graders," Tommy said. "We'll be in charge of the whole school and we'll get clapped out."

Tommy had two big brothers—twins Dante and Malik—who liked to tease him and us. The idea of being in charge must have made Tommy really happy.

"Ugh, let's not talk about next year," Josh said.

"It's summer vacation—baseball camp, soccer camp, and a whole month with my dad."

"What, no basketball camp?" Eddie joked.

"Maybe next year." Josh pretended to sink a basket.

"My dad's taking the summer off," I said. "Mom's going to teach summer school, so Kennedy's going to daycare every day. Dad and I will be home alone—it's going to be THE SUMMER OF DAD."

Whenever I said or even thought the words in my brain, THE SUMMER OF DAD came out in giant capital letters and in a big booming voice. I couldn't wait to find out all the fun things Dad had planned. Some of them would be history things. He and my mom both teach American history at the college, which is why my sister and I and even our family dog are named after presidents. But Dad and I biked to the state park and camped out last month with Tommy, Eddie, Josh, and Josh's dad. I was sure we'd do manly things like that—with no Mom to remind us to change our underwear and no four-year-old girl to make us play tea party.

I started a list of fun things in a notebook I titled **THE SUMMER OF DAD**. I knew Dad would have more exciting things to add:

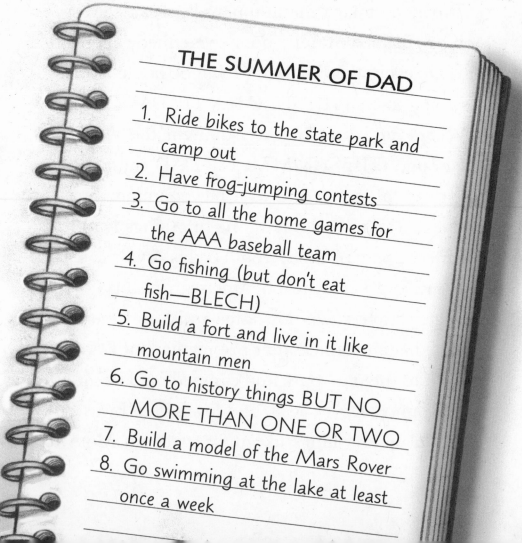

THE SUMMER OF DAD

1. Ride bikes to the state park and camp out
2. Have frog-jumping contests
3. Go to all the home games for the AAA baseball team
4. Go fishing (but don't eat fish—BLECH)
5. Build a fort and live in it like mountain men
6. Go to history things BUT NO MORE THAN ONE OR TWO
7. Build a model of the Mars Rover
8. Go swimming at the lake at least once a week

"Too bad you're going to be away all summer," I said to Josh. "My dad's going to take us fishing."

"Baseball and soccer camp are both at the high school," he answered. "So I'll be around on weekends. I'll be at my dad's in between, though."

"I'm going to try out for the play at the community theater," Tommy said shyly.

"Community theater?" Josh asked with a laugh. "Who's making you do that?"

"I may not get a part." Tommy stared at his shoes. "It's *The Sound of Music.*"

His cheeks were red, and I tried to make up for Josh laughing. "You'll get a part. You're a great singer!"

That was true. Tommy got a pretty big part as one of Peter Pan's lost boys in the school play even though he wasn't a fifth-grader.

"I thought you'd be able to hang out over the summer," I said.

"It'll be you and me, dude!" Eddie gave me a high five. "We've got our summer job."

I nodded, but being with Eddie all summer wasn't like being with Tommy. Eddie could be *work*. That kid loved trouble.

That's why we had gotten our job at Mrs. Crawford's in the first place. Eddie and Millard Fillmore—my dog, not the dead president—accidentally on purpose knocked over our neighbor's rabbit hutch, and her three bunnies nearly got eaten by the Dobermans next door.

As punishment, Eddie and I were helping Mrs. C. take care of her rabbits. People get bunnies for Easter presents and when they get bored of them, they bring them to an animal shelter. Some people even let their tame rabbits go free to be eaten by wild animals. Which is really messed up. Mrs. Crawford pays to have them fixed so that they can't have babies and tries to find them homes.

Eddie and I feed the rabbits, clean their cages, and make sure they have water. We had a booth at Field Day to raise money for them, but the booth kind of backfired when someone left two rabbits in a cage on Mrs. Crawford's front porch. I named them Neil Armstrong and Buzz Aldrin after the first two men who walked on the moon, but Armstrong turned out to be a girl—a *pregnant* girl.

"C'mon, hurry," I said. "Let's see if Armstrong had her babies yet."

She hadn't, but we still had three rabbits to feed and water, and three cages to clean out. Even with Josh's and Tommy's help, that was a lot of rabbit poop!

"Why are they in separate cages?" Josh asked.

"Mrs. C. has to keep them apart until we make sure the new rabbits don't have any diseases that will make Flopsy sick," I said.

"Rabbit zombies," Eddie said. He lurched around with a strange little bunny hop. Zombies were Eddie's favorite thing. He'd be King of the Zombies if he could.

When we finished, Tommy's father's pickup truck

was pulling into my driveway. Our dads and Tommy's brothers hopped out and started unloading a bunch of stuff into my garage.

"Is your dad making something?" I asked Tommy. His dad was an architect and great at building things. He even made a new rabbit hutch for Mrs. C. The twins tried to make an elevator out of spare bike parts so the bunnies would have a two-story penthouse, but it freaked Flopsy out.

"Not *my* dad." Tommy's cheeks were red again. "Yours. My dad's helping."

"Mine?" I asked. Ask my Dad who our 21st president was and he'd answer Chester A. Arthur without thinking—even though Arthur was only a one-term president that got the job after someone shot James Garfield. But building things? Not my dad's strong point.

"What's he doing?" I asked.

"The attic," Tommy said. "They're going to finish it—turn it into a real room."

The attic?

Dread washed over me like it did when my name was called over the loudspeaker with instructions to report to the principal's office. "That's where the ghosts live. That's why we call it THE ATTIC OF DOOM."

"Bad luck, dude." Eddie zombie-walked toward me. "They let those ghosts out of there and there's no telling what will happen."

I felt sick to my stomach. Was Dad going to be too busy dealing with ghosts to do anything fun at all? What about THE SUMMER OF DAD?

CHAPTER TWO
The Summer of Ghosts

I tried to warn Dad about the ghosts, but he was busy looking over plans Mr. Williams had rolled out on the hood of his truck.

"Go play with your friends, Roosevelt," Dad said. "I'll tell you all about it over dinner."

"Yeah, go and *play*," Dante said.

"*Children* shouldn't be around construction stuff," Malik added.

"Like you two are grown-ups," Tommy said. "You're in sixth grade."

"*Seventh* in September," Dante answered. "That's two years more grown up than you"

Mr. Williams stared at the twins with his *I Mean Business* face. "You, too," he said to the twins. "We're done unloading. Go home."

Eddie snickered and gave Tommy a secret high five. But the twins pushed past us, knocking us out of their way.

"Roosevelt, Millard Fillmore could use a walk. Get a snack and head out," Dad said.

"C'mon guys," I muttered.

When we got inside Fillmore, our Border Collie, jumped around, making sure to give us each a good sniff and a lick.

"Hi, boys!" Mom called from the kitchen. "How was—"

"What's Dad doing in the attic?" I asked, cutting her off. "He's going to let the ghosts out."

"Roosevelt," Mom said, taking in a big breath. Grown-ups do that a lot. It's like they don't get enough air with regular breaths. Teachers took loud breaths all the time, especially when I asked a lot of questions. "There's no such thing as ghosts."

Josh and Tommy were too polite to argue with

her, but not Eddie.

"I heard all kinds of noises coming from up there the last time I slept over," he said. "*Ghost* noises."

"That was a dream, or our old house creaking, or squirrels running on the roof. Not ghosts," Mom said.

Tommy's brothers told us that ghosts like to slip into live people's bodies while we're breathing in— so they can walk around and eat food and do other things that ghosts can't do. Sometimes a ghost will be walking around in your body for days and you won't even know it. I always make sure to breathe out really hard when I run past the door to THE ATTIC OF DOOM.

Mom shook her head again. Like she knew better than we did but wasn't going to argue. Grown-ups do that a lot too. "I made Great Grandma's sugar cookies to celebrate the last day of school. Dig in."

She poured glasses of milk while we grabbed cookies. Fillmore sat at our feet, hoping for crumbs.

Eddie wanted to make a bet about when the bunnies would be born, and the word bunnies drew my four-year-old sister Kennedy upstairs from the family room.

"Are baby bunnies here?" she asked.

"Not yet," I told her. "Maybe tomorrow."

"Can I see?"

"I'll take you after dinner," I told her. "The guys and I are going to walk Fillmore now."

That little word was all it took for Fillmore to bark and dance around looking for his leash. That dog liked to patrol the neighborhood and sniff every single bush.

All the way around the block while Josh talked about baseball camp and Tommy told us the story of *The Sound of Music* and Eddie pretended to be a zombie hungry for our brains, I worried about what Dad was planning to do to the attic. He and Mom sometimes said they'd like to have a real office instead of the corner of the living room so they could get away from the noise. But the attic was just a big, dusty space. There was plywood on the floor and the walls were flimsy, too. One creepy bare light bulb hung down from the slanted ceiling.

One day I'd come home to find Mom and Dad and maybe even Kennedy acting all weird because ghosts had taken over their bodies. I'd be the only normal person left in my whole family because there was no way I was spending time up in that attic, that's for sure.

Unless I could talk them into leaving the attic alone, THE SUMMER OF DAD was going to turn into THE SUMMER OF GHOSTS.

CHAPTER THREE
Babies are Slimy

We had pizza out on the back deck to celebrate the last day of school. I slipped my crusts to Fillmore when no one was looking. Every time I asked about the attic Mom or Dad changed the subject.

"Why don't you take Kennedy to see the rabbits," Mom said. "When you come back we'll have dessert and a family meeting."

Saying the word *rabbit* in front of Kennedy was like saying the word *walk* in front of Fillmore.

"Bunnies!" Kennedy jumped up and down, clapping.

But the words *family meeting* were the ones bouncing around my brain. Those words usually meant I was in trouble for something and would get called

Roosevelt Theodore Banks a whole bunch of times.

I kind of wanted to know what I had done wrong and get it over with, but Kennedy wouldn't calm down until she got a dose of bunny love. She skipped beside me, holding my hand when we crossed the street.

"Look both ways," she reminded me.

"Always. That's the rule," I answered. "And what's another rule?"

"Don't hug the bunnies too hard."

"Yes, and also you're never to cross the street by yourself. No matter how much you want to see the bunnies."

"I can when I'm big," she answered.

"Yes, but you're not—" Our feet touched the grass in Mrs. C.'s yard, and Kennedy shot off before I finished my sentence.

The urge to reach out and touch the new rabbits was so strong that she clasped her hands behind her back in front of Armstrong's and Aldrin's cages.

They didn't like to be touched, at least not yet, but Flopsy and Kennedy had become good friends. I opened the door to the hutch and Kennedy sat on the edge. A second later Flopsy hopped into her lap and rubbed her head under my sister's hand to get her to start petting. Pretty soon that bunny was purring like she was a cat.

My eyes were on Armstrong. That rabbit was definitely acting strange. She grunted and then turned her back on us with a growl. The next thing I knew, there was a slimy black ball in the nest she had created out of hay in her cage.

Mrs. C.'s back door was open so I ran up and yelled through the screen. By the time we made it back, there were two more slimy balls in the nest, and one more was on its way. We held our breaths, watching Armstrong grunt and move as more babies came. We counted six slime balls before she was finished.

YUCK. Bunny babies are gross.

Armstrong agreed. She hopped across the cage

and turned her back on them.

Kennedy was way more interested. She took such a long time watching those slimy bunny babies that Mom and Dad had to come and get us.

"We've got ice cream cake waiting for you two to celebrate the last day of school," Mom said. "And now new bunny babies to celebrate, too."

That's when I remembered—*family meeting*. But Mom had used the word *celebrate*. Did that mean I wasn't in trouble?

It was hard pulling Kennedy away from those babies.

"Armstrong," Kennedy ordered. "Take care of your babies."

"Rabbits stay away from their kits—their babies— for the first few days," Mrs. C. told her. "They come back once or twice a day to feed them. Baby bunnies don't have a strong scent, and mommies don't want to attract prey animals like skunks or raccoons to the nest. So they stay away except for feeding time."

Kennedy didn't seem convinced, or maybe it was the idea of skunks and raccoons that was troubling her.

"Don't worry," Mrs. C. continued. "Armstrong is being a good mommy. And the kits don't need a lot of attention. They'll be hopping around in no time."

It was only that and a promise that I would bring

Kennedy back to see the babies the next morning that convinced her to head home. If it was up to her, she'd set up a sleeping bag next to the rabbit cage and spend the night, ready to do battle with hungry skunks and raccoons.

When we were finally sitting around the picnic table with our ice cream cake, I waited to hear what I was in trouble for.

Mom and Dad looked each other in the eyes and did their parent mind-meld thing. Mom's lips were twitching like she was trying really hard not to laugh.

That's when Dad got ready to lower the boom. "We have good news—"

"Good news?" I asked. "I'm not in trouble?"

"What makes you think you're in trouble?" Mom asked. "I didn't get any calls from school today."

"Family meeting," I said. "Those are usually about me."

Dad shook his head. "This meeting isn't about you—well, not really. But you are a great big brother and that's one of the things we want to talk about."

Mom reached out and took one of my hands and one of Kennedy's into hers. I didn't point out that this was going to make my ice cream cake hard to eat, mostly because I liked when it melted into ice cream soup.

"You're going to be a big brother again, and Kennedy's going to be a big sister—"

"Baby bunnies!" Kennedy crowed, hopping up and down in her seat.

"Not bunnies," Dad told her. "A baby sister."

"A *human* baby? I asked.

Dad nodded.

"Yuck!" I knew about human babies. Aunt Jessica had one over the winter and let me tell you—the smells coming out of that baby's diaper were enough to attract raccoons, skunks, even bears. It would get eaten in half a second out in the wild. Mom was always going on about how cute it was, but it had a squished-up, ready-to-cry face every time I looked at it. *Double yuck!*

"A baby girl," Mom added. "In September."

"Baby girl!" Kennedy squealed.

"Another girl?" I blurted out. Now I was really disgusted. "Can't we at least get a boy?" It was going to be one long tea party at our house. All the more reason why Dad and I needed to have a super great, manly summer and why he should leave the attic alone.

"We don't get to choose boy or girl, Roosevelt," Dad said.

"I thought you had guessed," Mom said to me. "I saw you looking at my baby bump the other day."

I stared at Mom's stomach now like it was my enemy. I had noticed it was getting bigger, but I'd never guessed baby. "I thought you were getting fat," I muttered.

"Roosevelt!" Dad said. His voice had that warning tone. But instead of yelling at me, he took one of those big old person's breaths and changed the subject.

"We need to keep up our tradition by naming your new sister after a president."

"George Washington!" Kennedy shouted. That was the only president she knew.

I ran through a list of presidents' last names in my head.

"I'm thinking Taylor, for Zachary Taylor," Dad said. "Or Carter, for Jimmy Carter."

"No one remembers Zachary Taylor," I replied.

Dad liked President Carter because he was always building houses for people. He would be happy if I voted for Carter. "Carter," I said.

Dad smiled. "I'm leaning toward Carter, too."

Mom sighed and patted her belly. "I guess this is baby Carter, then. But her middle name will not be Jimmy."

Dad laughed. He had tried to name my sister Kennedy *John* Banks because I was Roosevelt *Theodore* Banks, but Mom wouldn't let him. Kennedy's middle name was Jane. Carter's would have to be another J name.

"So, are we happy about the new baby?" Mom asked. "Baby Carter?"

"Happy, happy, happy," Kennedy said. "I want the baby now."

"Just three months to wait," Mom said. "Carter needs more time in Mommy's belly before she's ready to be born."

"Like bunnies!" Kennedy said.

Mom laughed. "Yes, like bunnies. But I'm only having one baby. Not six."

"And one more thing," Dad added.

Uh oh, I thought. *Here comes the thing I'm in trouble for.*

"We're going to turn your bedroom into a nursery for baby Carter, Roosevelt. You'll move upstairs to a great new room in the attic."

"The attic?!" I jumped to my feet "You want me to move into THE ATTIC OF DOOM? With GHOSTS?"

CHAPTER FOUR
A Ghostly Tale

I ran to my room, slamming the door behind me. There was no way I was moving into THE ATTIC OF DOOM just so a slimy new baby could take my place.

I slumped into my desk chair, which wasn't on wheels and didn't spin around. Just saying. Everything else was just the way I liked it. I had my bed with the stars and moons and planets hanging from the ceiling. The bulletin board over my desk was covered with my science-fair blue ribbons, pictures of me and my friends, and one of Dad and me roasting marshmallows for s'mores over the fire on our camping trip.

Let the new baby sleep in the attic, I thought. *Ghosts*

can't cause too much trouble in a baby's body. Babies can't even walk.

There was an application on my desk for a summer writing program at the library with a famous author. Mom wanted me to try to get in. It would be cool to learn about writing from a famous author, but I was planning to be too busy with THE SUMMER OF DAD. Now he'd be the one who was too busy—too busy getting ready to feed me to ghosts.

I'll write a story that will be so good it will convince Mom and Dad that the ghosts are real and they'll leave the attic alone.

THE HOUSE OF DOOM
by Roosevelt Theodore Banks

One day, an orphan boy named Lincoln came home to find his evil aunt and uncle waiting for him at the door.

"We don't want you here anymore. You are going to live next door," his uncle said.

"We moved your bed, your clothes, and your one broken toy to the house's porch," his aunt added. "There is nothing for you here."

"But that house is haunted," Lincoln said.

"Too bad." His aunt cackled like a wicked witch. "I guess the ghosts will haunt you and move into your body."

Lincoln's knees shook. His teeth chattered. He was more scared than he had ever been, but his aunt and uncle would not change their minds. No one alive had been in the haunted house for years and years. The ghosts scared everyone away. These ghosts were a family of an old man and an old woman and their evil teenaged twins, Dante and Malik.

Lincoln's aunt and uncle locked him out of their house during a blizzard. Shivering, he dragged his bed into THE HOUSE OF DOOM. He wrapped a scarf around his mouth so the ghosts couldn't slip into his body while he slept. But ghosts are clever and tricky. When Lincoln woke up the scarf was gone, and he was sharing his body with the ghosts of both twins.

The twins fought over who would control Lincoln's body. Dante pulled him one way. Malik pulled him another. They threw him into walls, made him trip over his feet, and knocked him down the stairs. Lincoln was covered in bumps and bruises.

Mom and Dad stuck their heads in after they put Kennedy to bed to see how I was doing.

"Want to talk about it, buddy?" Dad asked.

I shook my head. My story would convince them that the attic was the worst idea ever, but I had to wait until it was perfect.

"Working on your story for the library?" Mom asked.

I nodded.

"Let's leave the mad genius to his creation," Mom

told Dad. "Lights out in an hour," she said to me.

I nodded again. My brain was thinking, thinking, thinking. I needed to come up with the perfect ending.

The poor orphan boy kept exhaling like he was blowing out candles on a really old person's birthday cake, but Dante and Malik wouldn't leave his body. They liked being able to move around in the world again and eat ice cream.

Lincoln asked the old man and old lady ghosts to make the twins leave his body, but they didn't want Dante and Malik hanging around either.

The twins got mad and so they did the most disgusting things they could think of in ~~Roosevelt's~~ Lincoln's body. Malik forced Lincoln to eat fish and lima beans. And Dante made him run after a girl who lived down the street and give her a big kiss right on the lips. Gross and grosser.

It turned out that Lincoln was allergic to fish

and to kissing girls. He died, and the next thing he knew he was a ghost, too. He moved in to his aunt and uncle's house and haunted them. They never had another day of peace.

THE END

When I finished, I typed it all into the computer and made sure there were no spelling errors and junk like that. Mrs. Anderson always said we had to revise our work to make it better, so I reread my story. It was brilliant and I didn't see any way to improve it—except with pictures.

I printed out two copies, added pictures to each, and stapled them together like real books. Then I left both copies on the kitchen table. My parents would sit down over breakfast, read my masterpiece, and realize what a big mistake they were making.

That would be the end of me moving into THE ATTIC OF DOOM.

Problem solved.

Fillmore followed me back to my bedroom and jumped up in bed with me like he always did. At least he was loyal. I fell asleep to the sound of him snoring his doggie snores.

CHAPTER FIVE
Waiting

The next morning I opened the back door to let Fillmore out so he could make his morning inspection of his backyard territory. There was always the risk that some other dog—or worse, cat—had moved in overnight. He sat on his hind legs, sniffing, and then took off like a shot, barking, when a squirrel had the nerve to think it could scamper up one of his trees.

Inspection completed, it was time for breakfast. I scooped some dog food into his bowl and checked his water before reaching for my own box of cereal.

Mom and Dad were at the table, drinking coffee and reading books. My story was sitting where I had left it.

Did they see it? Did they read it? Were they ready

to apologize for even thinking that I should move in with ghosts to make room for a new baby that was going to be all slimy and gross?

My parents were big on quiet in the morning. No TV first thing, no loud talking, and none of what they called pestering until AFTER their first cup of coffee.

I was about to break that rule when Kennedy looked up from her coloring book to ask when we could go see the baby bunnies and could we go now please?

She had dressed up for the bunny birthday. She wore a pink tutu over her yellow plaid shorts, a multi-colored polka-dot top, and every single plastic necklace she could find. There were bunny and butterfly and cat clips in her hair along with her birthday tiara.

I waited for Mom and Dad to tell her to be quiet, to let me eat my cereal, to inform her that their brilliant, creative, ghost-free son had better things to do that morning—like celebrate the fact that he wasn't moving into the attic.

"Let's let Roosevelt eat his breakfast first," Mom said.

I sat in my regular place with Fillmore at my feet waiting for anything that might drop. Kennedy watched me just as carefully, waiting for me to finish. Silently, Dad passed me my book about space exploration.

I waited for Mom or Dad to say something about my story.

I waited all through my cereal.

I waited all through my orange juice.

I waited all through Dad's harrumphing over whatever boring junk he was reading and Mom's note-taking from her own boring junk.

I waited for one of them to tell me that they had seen the light and I wouldn't have to move to THE ATTIC OF DOOM.

I waited and waited until I couldn't wait anymore.

"Hello!" I said. "Are we going to talk about THE ATTIC OF DOOM?"

Dad looked up at me, as calm as could be. "Take your sister to see the rabbits first. Then we'll talk."

"Go put your shoes on, sweetie," Mom said to Kennedy.

I harrumphed all the way to my ghost-free room and got dressed.

When I came out, Kennedy had added even more to her outfit. Her left wrist was covered with bright, plastic bracelets and she had a princess lollipop ring on her right hand.

Even though my life was hanging in the balance, I had to admit it was kind of cute the way she dressed up for those bunnies.

She took my hand and skipped across the street, breaking into a run the minute our feet touched Mrs. Crawford's grass. The babies were sleeping in a pile, and Armstrong watched from the other side of the cage.

Even though Eddie Spaghetti wouldn't be here until later, I got started cleaning the rabbit hutch and Buzz Aldrin's cage while Kennedy talked to the babies the way grown-ups talk to human babies—with a high-pitched voice and lots of silly sounds that don't mean anything. If it was going to be like this when the human baby came, my head might explode. That's if the ghosts didn't explode it first.

Tommy came out to help, and I was telling him about THE ATTIC OF DOOM when Dante and Malik wandered over.

"What are you losers doing?" Dante asked.

"Roosevelt's moving into the attic with the ghosts when the new baby comes," Tommy said.

Malik slapped me on the back, hard enough to make me drop the dirty hay I was carrying to the compost bin. "Too bad, kid. It was nice knowing you."

Tommy rolled his eyes. "When does baseball camp start already?" he asked.

"Monday," Dante answered. "The same day you start singing and dancing." He twirled across the yard and stood in front of Armstrong's cage with Kennedy. "Nice outfit," he said, giving Kennedy a fist bump. Kennedy wasn't sure if she was being teased or not. He stuck his fingers in the cage and tried to pet the babies. Armstrong leapt at him with a growl.

Dante jumped back, startled.

Malik laughed at him. "Scared of a little bunny, dude?" He stuck his own hands in the cage next, wiggling his fingers while Armstrong growled and kept her body between his fingers and the babies. I don't know if the babies thought danger was near or they smelled their mother and were hoping for breakfast. They started mewling.

Kennedy crossed her arms and glared at him. "Leave the baby bunnies alone."

"You going to beat me up?" Malik asked.

"Beat him up, Kennedy!" Dante laughed. He

danced around jabbing his fists like he was boxing. He danced right up to the other side of Armstrong's cage and tried to pet the babies.

Poor Armstrong didn't know what to do, so she sat there shaking and honking.

"Are you a goose or a rabbit?" Malik asked.

Kennedy didn't clam up or slink away like Tommy and I did when the twins were acting up. She stomped her foot. "You leave the bunnies alone," she said again. If she was a cartoon there would be smoke coming out of her ears. "Go away."

Malik raised his hands in surrender and backed up. Dante did the same.

"I don't like you, you're mean!" she yelled after them.

They chuckled, but I was impressed. Kennedy could sure be brave.

"Don't worry bunny rabbits. The mean boys are gone," she said, loud enough for them to hear.

It took me another fifteen minutes and a promise

to bring her back after lunch AND after dinner to convince her to go back home.

"Let's meet up when Eddie Spaghetti gets here," I said to Tommy. "Hopefully Mom and Dad have changed their minds and I won't be ghost food the next time you see me."

CHAPTER SIX
Bribes are Illegal

When we got back to the house, Dad pulled out plans for the attic room. "We're going to start by putting in a bigger, double window," he said. "You'll be able to look right across the street to Tommy's house. You can use flashlights to talk to each other in Morse code."

"I don't know Morse code," I said.

"I'll teach you. It's named after the inventor of the telegraph machine, Samuel—" Dad was about to drone on with some boring history junk.

Mom tapped his hand. "We're going to make your new room really nice," she said.

"Nice and creepy," I said.

"Roosevelt, I want you to listen and look at the

plans," Dad said. "There will be room for two beds. You can have sleepovers with Tommy or Eddie or Josh without anyone having to sleep on the floor."

"Except if they *all* want to sleep over," I said. Then I remembered. *Like anyone's going to want to sleep over with ghosts.*

"And lots of open floor space for games," Mom added.

Ghost tag? Checkers with the dead?

"Roosevelt, are you listening?" Dad asked.

I nodded.

"Mr. Williams showed me how we can build dresser drawers right into the wall." He pointed to some lines on the page.

Will they be big enough for me to hide in them?

"And a desk, too," Mom said, "where you can create your art and your stories."

Ghost stories.

"What do you say? Looks pretty good, doesn't it?" Dad said.

"Why can't you stick the new baby up there if it's going to be so great?" I asked.

Her baby stink and slime might drive the ghosts away.

"Roosevelt," Mom said. "Babies need to be fed and changed in the middle of the night, and they cry a lot. The baby needs to be on the same floor as us."

"I bet Kennedy would love to move up to the attic," I said.

I heard the sound of cartoons drifting up from the family room and felt bad for a minute. But not bad enough to volunteer to live with ghosts.

"Kennedy needs to be downstairs with us, too," Dad said. "You're the oldest. You get the best room. The attic bedroom is going to be big. Room for all your friends. Room for all of your hobbies. It's going to be great."

"Great for ghosts. Say goodbye to your son Roosevelt because there are going to be all kinds of ghosts roaming around in my body. I bet they might even eat fish. Gross!"

Mom pressed her lips together like she was holding in a laugh.

"They could eat something I'm allergic to and I could *die*."

"Roosevelt, you aren't allergic to any foods," Mom said.

I shook my head. "Fish," I muttered. "Lima beans."

"Those are things you don't like. They won't kill you."

Dad reached into his back pocket and dropped a small wrapped box in front of me. "Your mom and I have been talking, and we decided you're ready for some freedom. I'll be busy refinishing the attic, and Eddie will be here a lot to help with the rabbits. So we'll need a way to stay in touch with you."

I tore off the wrapping paper. "A cell phone!"

"A cell phone," Mom said. "You can't go online with it. And you can only call or text numbers we've already programmed in: Tommy, Eddie, Josh, Dad, and me. And 9-1-1."

"9-1-1 only in real emergencies," Dad said.

I stared at the phone like it might bite me. "Is this a bribe?" I asked. "Bribes are illegal, you know."

Mom sighed. "You've been asking for a phone for a long time. Aren't you excited?"

I *was* excited, but I wasn't ready to let them see that.

"You'll have a lot more freedom now that you have a phone," Dad said.

"Freedom?"

"We've been talking it over with Tommy's and Eddie's parents—"

"Not Josh's?"

"Josh will be busy or away most of the summer. But we can talk to his mother, if you want us to."

I nodded. Josh would want to be able to hang out with us on weekends. And he already had a phone.

"You boys can ride your bikes on the old railroad trail. It runs right behind the library and the convenience store and goes past the town pool."

"We get to go by ourselves?" I asked. The four of us had ridden our bikes on the railroad trail when we were training for our bike trip, but we were only allowed to go as far as the library without a grown-up.

"With your friends. Never alone. Use the buddy system. And you have to let Dad or me know where you're going and when you'll be back," Mom said. "Always wear your helmets, and bring your phones."

"And if Mom or I call you, you have to pick up," Dad said. "No matter what you're doing."

"What if I'm going to the bathroom? Or my mouth is full?"

"Pick up in a reasonable amount of time," Dad said.

I eyed the two of them, not quite believing what I was hearing. "You're really going to let us go to the pool by ourselves?" The pool wasn't as far or as big as the lake at the campground, but it was still water.

"Only if there are two or more of you, and you have to swim near one of the lifeguard stations," Dad said.

"And if I hear even a whisper that you're getting into trouble or causing trouble, then you'll lose that privilege," Mom said.

Does that mean no dunking? No cannonballs? It was better not to ask.

"With freedom comes responsibility— responsibility to follow the rules and keep yourself safe," Dad said.

"How does that sound?" Mom asked.

It sounds like Dad wants me out of his way this summer. That new baby isn't even here yet and she's already ruining everything.

I didn't say that out loud. Freedom and responsibility were bribes to get me to move in with ghosts. I slumped in my seat. My parents weren't going to listen to logic. I'd have to find another way to convince them or have my body taken over by ghosts.

CHAPTER SEVEN
Mountain Men

I looked over my SUMMER OF DAD list and said goodbye to all the fun things that were never going to happen. But the list gave me an idea. As soon as Eddie's mom dropped him off, I texted Josh and Tommy:

it's Roosevelt

i got a phone

emergency meeting @Tommy's

It was pretty exciting to be able to text instead of having to go and get Josh and then head to Tommy's house. There were three dots under my text. Someone was texting back!

on my way

It was Josh. Tommy chimed in a couple of seconds later.

When we were all together I told them all about the new baby—a girl—and being forced to live in the ATTIC OF DOOM with the ghosts.

"I'm going to have to move out of my house, or say goodbye to your friend Roosevelt because I'm going to be someone else soon—some ghost."

"Bad luck, man," Eddie said. "It was nice knowing you."

"I'd invite you to live with me," Tommy said, "but Dante and Malik ruined my parents to the idea of any more kids. I'm lucky I was born before they started to cause too much trouble."

"I've got an idea," I said. "Let's build a fort, and I'll live there. But not in my backyard. That might not be far enough away."

"In the woods?" Tommy asked.

"Yeah. When my parents see that I mean business, they might come to their senses, or I can live there like a mountain man."

"Cool," Eddie said. "It can be our bike dudes clubhouse, too."

We raced to the small patch of woods at the end of our street. There was a humongous tree that was great for climbing about ten feet from the railroad trail. Dante and Malik had tried to build a tree house in it once, but they never finished. I found a piece of plywood under a pile of old leaves and pulled it underneath the tree.

"Here's our floor," I said.

Tommy looked around. "We're going to need more stuff if we're going build walls and a roof. Dad's always got extra building materials. We can look in my garage."

"We should make a plan, too—a blueprint," I said.

Eddie grabbed a stick. He and Josh made a kind of blueprint on the top of a big, flat rock, using sticks and leaves for walls and a roof while Tommy and I checked the woods to see if there was more stuff we could use.

"We won't need to make a door," Eddie said. "We can leave one side open, since it's summer."

"Right," I agreed. "We can wait and put that side in before winter comes. And blizzards." *I'll be back in my old room long before winter—and blizzards. Mom and Dad will come to their senses.*

Mom texted to let me and Eddie know it was time for lunch.

"Let's meet at Tommy's in an hour," I said. Then I remembered I had made a promise to Kennedy. "Wait, make that an hour and a half—I have to take my sister to see the baby bunnies."

"The babies were born?" Eddie asked.

"I saw them this morning. They're cute," Tommy said.

"You should have seen them when they came out. Gross and slimy," I told them. "I can't believe I'm getting another human one at home."

"You don't want another Kennedy hanging

around?" Josh said. "She's not so bad."

None of the other guys had kids younger than they were in their families. Josh and Eddie didn't have any siblings at all. For half a second, I felt lucky. Then I remembered—new baby equals living with *GHOSTS*.

We spent Saturday afternoon—after Kennedy looked at the bunnies for a loooong time—gathering materials for the fort. I borrowed Kennedy's red wagon, which she used as a princess bus for her dolls, to haul the stuff down the street. Sunday was building day. We nailed some old boards together to make two walls. A giant piece of plywood would be the third.

"Should we try to make a window?" Josh asked.

I shook my head. "We'd need a saw, and no way our parents would let us use one. Besides, we can leave the fourth wall off until winter."

"We do have to figure out how to make a roof—for

rainy days," Tommy said.

"Hey!" Josh yelled. "There's Mr. Casey."

Mr. Casey, one of the fifth-grade teachers, was riding his bike on the trail and stopped to check out our work. "Pretty good fort, boys."

"We're going to be mountain men," I told him.

He laid a hand on one of the walls and it wobbled but stayed upright.

"We need a roof, though," Tommy said.

Mr. Casey nodded. "Even mountain men have to find a way to keep the rain out. A tarp would do, if you can find one. Staple or lash it to the walls."

"Good idea," I said, like I knew what *lash* meant.

"And bring a waterproof box or cooler to store your important things, like your summer reading books."

Eddie snorted. He'd be calling me the night before school started to find out what books I read over the summer and what they were about.

Mr. Casey smiled at him. "Maybe you'll like

Hatchet by Gary Paulsen—it's about a boy who lives by himself in the wilderness with nothing but a hatchet for protection. Not even a cool fort like the one you've built."

Teachers were tricky that way, always trying to sneak some learning in, but I made a mental note to look for the book on my next visit to the library. It sounded kind of cool.

He looked around again. "You do need to be careful of bears though."

"Bears?" I asked.

"There've been a few spotted in the state park," he said. "If you see one, stay away."

"*Hungry* bears!" Eddie Spaghetti zombie-walked toward me. "I'm a bear and I eat mountain men."

"The woods were their home first. If you see a bear, move away slowly," Mr. Casey told us. "And move sideways. That doesn't threaten them. And whatever you do, don't get between a mama bear and her cubs. Mama bears will attack if they think their cubs are in danger."

Babies sure cause a lot of trouble, I thought.

"What else should we do?" I asked. My voice was high and squeaky. Not that I was afraid or anything.

"Don't leave food around, and make noise while you're out here." He climbed back onto his bike. "Bears don't want to see you any more than you want to see them. If they hear you, they'll stay away."

I watched him ride off. Suddenly I didn't know what was worse—bears or ghosts. But I wasn't ready to give up. I had to prove to my parents that I meant business about the attic. "Let's all sleep here tonight," I said.

Eddie shuffled backwards. "My mom won't let me." He checked the time on his phone. "She's picking me up soon and we're going to my cousins' house for a barbecue. And besides, dude—bears."

I turned to Josh. "What about you?"

Josh raised his eyebrows. "I start baseball camp tomorrow. No way my mom will let me."

"Are you sure? Ask her."

Josh eyed Tommy and Eddie, and then shook his head. "Dude, bears."

Tommy was my best and oldest friend in the world. There was no way he'd leave me to sleep outside in the woods by myself. But when I looked at him, he looked away.

"*The Sound of Music* auditions are tomorrow morning," he said. "I need to get a good night's sleep."

"You can sleep here. I won't keep you up," I told him.

Tommy shook his head.

He's scared. They're all scared, I realized.

"Maybe your Dad will sleep here with you," Tommy volunteered.

Now I was the one shaking my head. "He won't believe I'm moving out if I make him sleep here with me. I guess I'm on my own."

Eddie snorted. "You and the bears."

The four of us walked out of the woods and Josh peeled off toward his street. I didn't say a word as we made our way toward my house. Eddie's mom was pulling into my driveway.

"See you tomorrow," Eddie said, hopping into the back seat. "If you haven't been eaten by a bear."

CHAPTER EIGHT

My Dad the Criminal

That night at dinner I announced that I was going to be a mountain man and live in the woods. "Could you make me breakfast to bring with me, Mom?" I asked. "But nothing that smells, because I don't want to be eaten by a bear."

Mom raised her eyebrows. "A bear?"

Uh-oh, I shouldn't have mentioned bears.

"It's not really a problem. Mr. Casey said he's seen them in the woods, but I know exactly what to do if I see one. So I'll probably live—except if it eats me when I'm sleeping."

"Are Tommy, Josh, and Eddie planning to sleep out there with you? Did their parents give them permission?" Dad asked.

"They're all scared," I told him. "But I'm not. Not of bears. Only of ghosts. And Fillmore will come with me, won't you, boy?"

Fillmore wagged his tail a little bit, but he didn't seem sure. He liked my bed.

"You will not be sleeping in the woods by yourself," Mom said.

I tried not to look too relieved.

Dad gave her some kind of parent mind-meld signal with his eyes. "Let's take a look at this mountain-man camp you've built. Then we'll decide."

Dad? You really want to get rid of me, don't you?

After dinner I gathered my sleeping bag, my toothbrush, and a bottle of water. "See," I told Mom. "I'll be brushing my teeth even though I'm a mountain man now."

"Bunny time!" Kennedy announced.

"Bunnies and then mountain-man camp," I said.

We put Fillmore on his leash and headed out. Kennedy looked at those babies for about a million minutes. Mrs. C. finally said she would watch Kennedy while we walked Fillmore.

I led them all past the railroad trail to the fort.

"We're going to put a roof on soon—a tarp," I said. "But it's not going to rain tonight."

Dad put his hand on one of the walls and shook it like Mr. Casey did. "You boys did a good job," he said.

Is he really going to let me sleep out here?

Mom shot him a look.

"But I don't like—"

Just then a group of about ten people went by on bicycles, waving hello. Fillmore started barking and straining at his leash to run after them.

"Absolutely not," Mom said. "You're not sleeping out here with or without your friends. Not with all kinds of strangers riding past."

I didn't want her to see how happy I was about that, so I kicked the dirt and said, "Mooooommm, you're no fun."

"I'm no fun either," Dad said. "If you want to have a sleepover outside with your friends, we can set up the tent in our backyard. But you're not sleeping in the woods without a grown-up."

"Will you sleep out here with me, Dad?" I asked.

"Not tonight, buddy. I have a busy day tomorrow— I'm starting on the attic!"

I frowned, then had an idea. "Do you think the ghosts will fly out when you make the hole in the house for the new window?"

"I'm sure they will," Mom said. "Now let's go home."

That night, I lay in my bed listening to the creaks and moans and squeaks that came from the attic. And was that a whisper? I held my breath and strained my ears. It was. I couldn't make out the words, but there was definitely a whisper conversation happening up there. The ghosts were probably talking about how they'd be walking around and eating fish and lima beans in my body. Maybe even kissing girls—blech!

Uh-oh, what if Dad isn't safe from ghosts?

I knew ghosts liked kids better than grown-ups—Dante and Malik said so—but what if the ghosts went after Dad anyway?

I got out of bed and pulled my pajama top over my nose and mouth and went to the attic door. I listened to make sure the ghosts weren't right there waiting to pounce on me. They sounded like they were on the other side of the room. My whole body was trembling, but I had to save Dad. I opened the door—fast—locked it from the inside and closed it just as fast.

I tried the doorknob and it wouldn't turn.

Ha! There's no way Dad is getting in there tomorrow.

I woke up the next morning feeling groggy. I could tell by the sun shining through my window and how loud the birdsong was that I had slept late, probably because I stayed up listening to ghost whispers. Then

I remembered my brilliant idea to lock the attic door. Dad couldn't remodel the room if the door was locked from the inside, could he?

Except he could.

I slipped out of my bedroom to find the door to

the attic standing wide open. Dad was at the top of the stairs with his hands on his hips as if he had just won a game of King of the Mountain.

"What are you doing?" I asked with my pajama shirt over my nose and mouth. Dad didn't hear me. "What are you doing?" I repeated, louder this time.

"Morning, sleepyhead," Dad said. "Any idea how the attic door got locked?"

I stared at the floor so he wouldn't see my eyes. Parents always knew what you were thinking, especially when you were thinking things you didn't want them to know about. "The ghosts must have done it. They don't want you up there, I guess. Wait—" I said. "How did you get the door open? There's no keyhole on this side of the doorknob."

"One of the things we'll do before you move up here is get a new doorknob—one without a lock," he said. "I wouldn't want you to get trapped up here by accident."

"Are you a criminal?" I asked.

"A criminal?"

"You picked a lock. That's illegal."

"Lock-picking in your own house isn't illegal, and that's an easy lock to pick," Dad said.

I stared at him for a minute. One of the presidents must have been an expert lock-picker or something. How else would my dad know how to pick a lock?

"Have your breakfast and then go to Mrs. C.'s to take care of the rabbits. Kennedy and Mom already left for the college," he said. "It took Mom a long time to get Kennedy to leave the baby bunnies," he added with a chuckle.

"New babies take up a lot of time and attention, don't they? Not to mention people's private rooms."

Dad came and sat at the top of the attic stairs. He had a white mask hanging off one of his ears. "Babies do take a lot of time and attention in the beginning," he said. "But think about how much fun it will be to have a new baby around. We can teach her all kinds of things."

"Are you ever going to have fun with me again?" I asked. "Teach *me* things?"

He looked me in the eye for a long second. "Roosevelt, of course I am. You're my best buddy. Having a new baby isn't going to change that. It's not going to change how I feel about you. What *will* change is that for a little while, Mom and I are going to be distracted and busy with the new baby."

I frowned at him, but he couldn't see that because I still had my pajamas up over my mouth and nose. I wasn't taking any chances.

"And I know you're going to be a big help with Kennedy while all that's going on."

Kennedy will completely ignore me when the new baby comes, just like you, I thought. But I didn't say that. Instead I asked, "What are you doing up there today?"

"I'm getting started." He sounded excited. "I've got to pull out the paneling and the old insulation. You'll need new insulation before we put the walls up. Otherwise you'll be freezing this winter."

I grunted. *That's if I'm not dead.* "Are you doing that by yourself?"

"I can do this part myself. Mr. Williams is going to help me when he can. A carpenter's going to put in the drawers and desk and the window."

"What about me?" I asked. "I can help. If I wear one of those masks the ghosts won't be able to fly into my body."

"I don't want you breathing in all this insulation dust," Dad said. "Go grab breakfast. I'm sure Eddie will be here soon."

The next thing I knew, Dad put his white mask over his mouth and nose, donned a pair of work gloves, and started yanking the thin plywood off the walls.

I closed the door behind me, a giant knot in my stomach. It was really happening. He was going to turn THE ATTIC OF DOOM into a bedroom—*my* bedroom.

CHAPTER NINE
Skeletons in the Attic

A couple of hours later, Eddie and I were watching from Mrs. C.'s yard when a big truck came and dropped off a dumpster on the side of the house. Dad opened the small attic window and started throwing the old insulation down into it.

He saw us watching and waved us over. "I found some cool stuff hidden behind the wall boards! We'll check it out after lunch."

"What do you think he found?" I asked Eddie.

"Skeletons," he answered.

We were still watching when Tommy's mom pulled into the driveway and Tommy popped out of the car.

"Did you get a part?" I asked.

"I'll hear in a couple of days." He shrugged with a shy smile. "They said I was one of the best singers though."

"Come over for lunch," I said. "My dad found stuff in the attic."

"Skeletons," Eddie said.

Tommy turned pale.

"Not skeletons," I said. "We don't know what yet, but probably not skeletons"

Lunch with Dad was a lot different than lunch with Mom. He threw a loaf of bread and some lunch meat and cheese on the picnic table on the deck and we made our own sandwiches. There were chips, too, which Mom didn't usually allow.

Fillmore patrolled the yard to make sure no intruders had found their way in since this morning before settling at our feet.

Dad seemed excited, like he wasn't getting ready to hand me over to a bunch of ghosts.

"So what did you find?" I asked him.

"Skeletons?" Eddie asked.

"I did find a few bones," Dad admitted. "Probably a squirrel. I also found an old squirrel's nest and a bat."

"A living bat? A *vampire* bat?" I asked.

"No, a normal bat. I threw it out the window and it flew away. We'll have to figure out how they were getting in so that we can block their entry."

"Bats are going to be flying around my head along with ghosts?" I asked.

"No," Dad said. "We'll get it taken care of. And if you see a bat, don't touch it. Bats can carry rabies."

"*You* touched one," Tommy said, his eyes wide.

"I was wearing gloves and long sleeves. I'm fine."

"Rabies is deadly," Eddie said. "But first you turn into a kind of zombie and run around biting people with foam coming out of your mouth."

"No one's getting rabies," Dad announced. "Now look at the cool stuff I found. A flag with 48 stars! Imagine that. A flag that was made before Alaska and Hawaii became states. The people who lived in this house probably flew it over the front door on holidays."

The flag was dusty and kind of faded—more pink, gray, and lavender than red, white, and blue, but still cool I guess.

"There's more," Dad said.

"Skeletons?" Eddie asked again.

"A million dollars?" I asked. "If you found a million dollars we could move into a bigger house without any ghosts."

"No skeletons and no ghosts," Dad said. He pulled something out of his pocket like it was the most amazing thing ever. "John F. Kennedy campaign buttons," he announced.

One button read *Students for Kennedy*. The other said *Kennedy for President*. His picture was on them, too.

"There's a Kennedy/Johnson poster, but it's torn. I bet a student lived here—maybe a high-school or college kid—during the 1960 election and supported Kennedy. Isn't that cool?" he asked.

It *was* pretty cool, I guess. But more for my sister than for me.

"Did you find any Roosevelt stuff?" Tommy asked. "That would be *really* cool."

"No, no Roosevelt stuff. This house wasn't built yet when Teddy was president. Not even when Franklin was in office. It was built after World War II, during the Eisenhower years. Abraham Lincoln built a log cabin when he was a teenager."

He eyed each one of us, hoping we'd ask questions. We didn't. We all knew that once my dad started talking about presidents, it was hard to get him to stop.

He waited for another minute, then stood up, stretched, and said it was time to get back to work. "What are you guys up to this afternoon?"

"Let's go check on our mountain-man fort," I said to Tommy and Eddie. "See if any bears moved in overnight."

"Or pooped in it," Eddie said with a laugh.

"I found a tarp in my garage. We can use it for the roof," Tommy said, racing off to get it.

We made a lot of noise running into the woods in case of bears. I was happy to see our fort was still standing. We managed to stretch the tarp from one of the side walls to the other. Between the tree branches and the blue tarp overhead, we were in a kind of blue-green glow. But once we did that, there wasn't anything else to do.

Tommy was singing under his breath, and I could tell he would like to be at home, rehearsing. Eddie was throwing rocks at what looked like an old birds' nest in the branches above us, until two birds started dive-bombing his head.

"Zombie birds!" He ran away, screaming.

"That must be a new nest, not an old one." Tommy stood on his tiptoes. "There are baby birds inside. They're only protecting their babies."

"I thought they were trying to eat my brains." Eddie zombie walked back, flapping his arms like a demented bird. "Need brains for zombie babies."

I sighed. More babies causing trouble. "What happens to the old babies when new ones are born?"

"They fly away," Tommy said. "Long before the new ones come."

Probably that's what my parents are wishing I'll do.

My phone rang. It was Mom. "Kennedy's home," I told the guys. "She's asking to go see the bunnies."

I had to admit that the bunny kits were cuter now that they weren't slimy anymore. Kennedy kept trying to feed them carrots even though Mrs. C. told us that they wouldn't be ready to eat real food for another few weeks. Armstrong seemed happy about the extra food though. Poor Flopsy only got a pat or two before Kennedy turned back to the babies.

That's probably what Mom and Dad will be like with the new baby. The old kids—me and Kennedy—will be lucky to get a pat or two.

"What happens when the babies start eating on their own?" I asked Mrs. C.

"Bunny kits only stay with their mothers for about two months. But we'll wait until these kits can be neutered at about three months, and then we can adopt them out."

I thought about that for a minute. "And what

happens to the mother?"

"If she's in the wild, she can have a new litter pretty quickly. Rabbits have a lot of babies," Mrs. C. said.

"And they just forget about the old ones," I muttered. "Just like birds."

We were still watching the bunnies when Mrs. Williams drove up. Dante, Malik, and Josh all spilled out of her car.

"What's Josh doing with your brothers?" I asked Tommy.

"He's in baseball camp with the older kids, because he was so much better than the players our age."

"How was it?" I asked Josh when he walked over.

"Okay, I guess. They were picking on me a little, but I struck four of them out in practice." He started to grin. "Even Dante and Malik."

"Cool!" Tommy gave him a high-five.

"So what'd I miss?" Josh asked. "Any news on the ghosts?"

CHAPTER TEN

Eggs for the Fourth of July

Over the next two weeks I watched a big hole get cut into the side of the house and a new window put in. Some of Dad's friends came by from the college to help with things like new insulation and the new floor. Mr. Williams was the one to show Dad how to put up the walls. Dante and Malik helped with the heavy lifting.

"Check out the ghost situation," I told them. "I think maybe they left when they made that big hole in the side of the house for the new window."

"We'll let you know," Dante said.

An hour later, the twins made a big deal of taking their white construction masks off and stretching

like they had been working hard all day.

"Well?" I asked.

"Bad news." Dante shook his head. "The ghosts are still there."

"Good thing we were wearing our masks or I don't know who would be talking to you right now," Malik added.

Something heavy dropped in my stomach. "That's it. I'm a goner," I said.

"Maybe not. You could try a ghostbusting ceremony," Dante said.

"What's that?" I asked.

"Do things to get the ghosts to leave," Malik said.

"Like a battle to get rid of ghosts?" Josh asked. "I think I've heard of them."

"Yeah," Dante said. "You have to go to battle against the ghosts."

I thought about that for a minute. I didn't trust the twins, but they seemed to know a lot about ghosts.

"There are three things ghosts hate—slime, loud

noises, and really, really bad smells," Malik said.

"Really bad smells," Dante repeated.

"Hit them with all three of those things and those ghosts are goners," Malik said.

"It's worth a try." I turned to Tommy. "You in?"

He swallowed, but nodded. "I'll help."

"Eddie will, too," I said. "I know it without asking."

I eyed Josh.

"If I'm not at my dad's, I'm in," he said. "I leave on July fifth."

I breathed a big sigh of relief. Going into battle with ghosts would be a lot easier with my dudes at my side.

"So when will you do it?" Dante asked.

"There's no way my parents will let me. They don't even believe in ghosts," I said. I looked over my shoulder. Kennedy had a lap full of baby bunnies. She hadn't heard a thing.

Tommy stepped closer and lowered his voice. "What about the Fourth of July party? The whole neighborhood will be at my house. No one will notice if we slip away."

The Williams family held a big Independence Day bash in their backyard every year. Pretty much the whole neighborhood came, even the crabby people. Everybody brought things like big bowls of macaroni salad or hot dogs for the grill. Mom made potato salad and an ice cream cake every year. And I knew Dad would be bringing the flag and the Kennedy buttons he found in the attic.

"Good idea," I told him. "That gives us time to gather supplies. And if we wear those masks, we should be safe until the ghosts leave."

Malik shook his head. "You need to look those ghosts in the face."

"In the face? Are we going to see ghost faces?" My voice got high and screechy.

"It's the slime," Dante said. "You can see their faces in the slime."

"You can borrow our water blasters," Malik said.

"Fill them with slime and let the ghosts have it. You know how to make slime?"

I nodded. "Made it for a science thing once. It's easy. And we can play old people music—like opera ladies screeching," I said.

"Or *The Sound of Music*." Malik flicked Tommy on the back of the head. "Just have Tommy boy sing as loud as he does in the shower."

Tommy had gotten the part of Kurt, one of the kids. He was always singing the songs under his breath and doing dance moves when he wasn't at rehearsal.

"Cut it," Tommy said, pushing him away.

"What about smells?" Dante asked.

"I'll feed Fillmore a can of beans and bring him up there. Fillmore's farts will drive anything away."

"You need more than dog farts to get rid of ghosts. We've been cooking up some stink bombs—"

"Hey, you can't give those away," Malik said. "I have plans for those."

Dante pulled him aside and we could hear them arguing, but not what they were saying.

"We can let you have them," Malik said finally, "but it's going to cost you. I'm not giving them up for nothing."

"What do you want for them?" I asked.

"Twenty dollars," the twins said at the same time.

"Twenty dollars?!" I yelled. "You're crazy! I don't have twenty dollars."

"What do you have?" Dante asked.

I thought about what was in my piggy bank. Grandma and Grandpa had just sent me money for my good report card. I needed to buy the stuff to make slime, and I was saving up to buy a Mars Rover model. "I can pay you five dollars," I said.

Malik crossed his arms over his chest. "Not enough."

I could go up to ten, but I didn't want to. Homemade stink bombs from the twins? They probably wouldn't even work.

"Eight dollars. Take it or leave it," I said. "I probably don't even need your stink bombs. Fillmore's farts are pretty powerful."

The next thing I knew I was handing over eight dollars and Dante was handing me a plastic bag filled with four… eggs?

"What the—"

Dante pulled the bag away, but he had already put my money in his pocket.

"Those aren't just any eggs," Malik said. "We hid them behind the water heater in the basement in April. They've been slowly rotting there ever since. Crack those shells and there will be a mighty stink."

"A *mighty* stink," Dante repeated. "Like a thousand dog farts. Or the smell of Tommy's breath in the morning."

"Hand them over," I said, trying to sound tough.

Dante started to hand me the bag. Then he pulled it just out of my reach. He did that three or four more times before I finally had them in my hands.

"Keep them somewhere safe," he said. "You don't want them to fall into the wrong hands."

The next morning, I shared the plan with Eddie. As soon as we finished with the rabbits, I texted Dad that we were biking to the convenience store "for candy." We bought everything we needed to make slime and put it all in the fort.

"Where are the stink bombs?" he asked.

"In the back of one of my desk drawers," I told him. "As long as you don't break the shell, they don't smell."

"Maybe we should try one, just in case."

"No, better save them. We need as big of a stink as possible. Tommy's working on the music. He's going to download some opera lady singing. I'll use my mom's Bluetooth speaker."

Eddie nodded. "Are you sure we can't wear masks?"

"The twins said we have to look them in the face.

But just think—in a few days THE ATTIC OF DOOM will be ghost free."

"We can call it THE ATTIC OF DUDES," Eddie said.

I liked the sound of that. But it was still a big risk. And I wasn't just risking my own life. Tommy and Eddie were on the line, too. What if when we went back to the Fourth of July party, we had ghosts walking around in our bodies?

CHAPTER ELEVEN

D-Day

As soon as Eddie and I finished with the rabbits on the Fourth of July, I texted Tommy and Josh and we met at the fort.

While I mixed the slime and Eddie added green food coloring, Tommy played us the music he had downloaded. Some old-lady opera singer screeched in a really high voice in some other language.

"What's it about?" Josh asked.

"Love, probably," Tommy said.

Blech!

He set it to play over the speaker and turned the music up loud. Birds shot out of the trees and a squirrel ran for cover. If ghosts were anything like animals, they'd be running from that noise as fast

as they could.

We filled three water blasters with green slime and hid them and the speaker under my back deck. We were ready. I just had to wait until my parents were busy at the party.

"If there are still ghosts in THE ATTIC OF DOOM after all this, there's no getting rid of them— not ever," I said. There were butterflies crash-diving in my belly.

"It'll work." Josh put his fist out. "Operation Banish Ghosts."

"Operation Banish Ghosts," Tommy repeated, putting his fist next to Josh's.

Eddie and I did the same. The four of us bumped fists.

"Operation Banish Ghosts," I said.

We raised and separated our hands while we made the sound of a mini explosion.

Mom opened the back door to let Fillmore outside. She startled when she saw us.

"What are you four plotting so seriously?"

"Plotting?" My voice cracked.

Tommy's cheeks turned red and he stared at his shoes.

Josh threw a toy for Fillmore.

"Not plotting anything, Mrs. Banks," Eddie said brightly. "Just talking about the Fourth of July. Do you think Mr. Banks can tell us about the first Independence Day?"

"I don't think you can avoid it," Mom said with a laugh. "Roosevelt, have you seen the big bowl I use for potato salad?"

It was under the deck with the blasters, covered in gobs of green slime.

"Um, no," I said. "I don't see it." Technically that wasn't a lie because I wasn't looking at the bowl right at that minute.

Mom frowned. "It's disappeared."

I could feel the truth bubbling in my stomach, wanting to get out. If she asked again, I'd have to hand the bowl over and explain.

Don't ask again. Don't ask again. Don't ask again, I chanted in my head.

"Come up and help me carry these things over to Tommy's backyard," she said.

Whew! It worked.

By four o'clock everyone from the neighborhood had gathered at Tommy's. Mrs. Williams was making hot dogs and hamburgers on the grill while Mr. Williams set up games. Kennedy, of course, was next door in Mrs. C.'s yard with a pile of baby bunnies in her lap, and some of the party spilled over there.

Kennedy was clearly in charge when it came to who could pet those bunnies. She kept shooing Dante and Malik away.

Tommy, Eddie, Josh, and I ate our fill of hot dogs, hamburgers, and chips. We drank cans of orange soda really fast and then let out big mountain-man burps before going back for dessert.

"Some salad wouldn't hurt," Mom said. "Or fruit."

"It's a *holiday*," I told her. "I bet George Washington's mother didn't make him eat salad on the first Fourth of July."

"That's because he was fighting a war," Mom said.

That was all it took to get my dad started. He told a story about how George Washington's mother wrote to him when he was fighting in the French and Indian War to ask him to send her some butter. She had run out.

I have to admit that was pretty funny, but then Dad started in on July 4, 1776 and even the grown-ups' eyes started to glaze over. Mr. Williams asked about how the renovation was going as soon as he could get a word in, and pretty soon half the grown-ups were heading over to my house to check it out.

"I hope they don't stay too long," I whispered to Tommy.

It was already six o'clock and we definitely did *not* want to be banishing ghosts in the dark. And this might be the only afternoon that neither of my parents would be home before the room was finished and I had to move in.

To pass the time, we played cornhole.

I kept one eye on my house. The grown-ups finally came back outside, but they were standing around talking in my front yard.

I did not want to conduct Operation Banish Ghosts in the dark. And I wasn't sure Tommy, Eddie, and Josh would stick with me if I did.

Leave! Leave! Leave! I chanted in my head. After all, it worked with Mom and the potato-salad bowl. It didn't work now. It took those grown-ups *forever* to walk across the street. As soon as my front yard was empty, I signaled to my boys.

We slipped away one at a time like army men, dashing across the street and meeting up in my backyard.

I picked up the blasters and gave one each to Eddie, Tommy, and Josh. Tommy had his phone ready to go and I carried the speaker.

"Time for Operation Banish Ghosts," I said.

We climbed the steps to the deck, and I slid the back door open as quietly as I could so we could take the ghosts by surprise. Thank goodness Fillmore was at the party, or he'd be barking and jumping all over us.

We crept upstairs and I slipped into my room, grabbing the plastic bag of stink bombs from my desk.

The four of us stood in front of the attic door.

I could feel my heart beating fast and I think my hand was shaking. I held my fingers up and whispered, "When I say go."

Josh's lips were pressed tightly together. He raised his slime blaster. Eddie did the same. Tommy turned on his phone and started the music. A second later, I made the speaker volume as high as I could.

I slammed the door open and yelled, "Go! Go! Go!"

CHAPTER TWELVE
Operation Banish Ghosts

I threw the speaker up the stairs with the opera lady screaming her song. I ran up behind it and opened the plastic bag. I smashed one egg in my hand and threw it across the room.

Eddie, Tommy, and Josh were on my heels. They were blasting slime all around me, and Josh nailed a ghost right in the eyes! I saw the outline of its face for one second before the slime dripped to the floor and it disappeared. I threw the second egg and then the third, choking on the stench.

Let me tell you, that rotten-egg smell was worse than a million of Fillmore's farts combined. If I was a ghost, I'd fly out of that attic in a second.

The blasters were empty. The opera lady's song was coming to an end. I threw the last stink bomb as hard as I could and it smashed into the wall, dripping rotten egg down to the floor. I was sure I saw a shimmer by the windows. The ghosts were leaving.

I dashed over and slammed the windows closed so that they couldn't come back.

"Retreat!" I yelled. "Retreat!"

Eddie dropped his blaster and headed for the stairs.

Josh and Tommy were on his heels.

I was right behind them. I banged the door shut behind me.

The smell was so bad it followed us as we ran to the backyard. I thought I was going to throw up, but Eddie did instead. Right into the garbage can.

Gross!

"Who knew a couple of rotten eggs could smell *that* bad?" Josh said.

"That was a mighty stink." I slumped into the grass. My whole body shook and I felt sick to my stomach, but I was excited and happy at the same time. We had done it. We had banished the ghosts!

Tommy took deep breaths and swallowed a lot. "The was the worst smell I ever smelled," he said. "I can *taste* it, it was so strong."

"But did you see us with those ghost blasters?" Eddie asked. He pretended he was still holding it, blasting slime around.

Tommy did the same, and I was sorry that I hadn't done that, too. But the stink bombs were more important, even if they were less fun.

"I saw a ghost face!" I told them. "For one second before the slime dripped to the floor, I saw a ghost face!"

"I'm pretty sure I saw the back of one," Josh said.

"Me, too. I saw some shimmers by the window," I told him.

"I was never so scared in my whole life," Tommy

said. "And I live with Dante and Malik."

"Me, too," I agreed. "You guys are the best friends ever to do that with me."

"Operation Banish Ghosts is a victory," Eddie said, pumping his fist.

I threw my head back and shouted, "Victory! THE ATTIC OF DOOM is now THE ATTIC OF DUDES!"

"How long will that take for the mighty stink to go away, do you think?" Josh asked.

I shrugged. "By the time the party ends for sure."

"It followed us outside—the mighty stink," Tommy said.

I breathed in the clean summer air. But I kept smelling the stink bombs, too. I waved my hand to scare off a mosquito and it was even stronger. "My hands! My hands stink!"

I ran to the hose on the side of my house and rinsed my hands, but the smell didn't go away. There was a bottle of bubbles that Kennedy and I played with a couple of days ago. I poured it onto my hands and scrubbed them like the bubbles were soap. It took three or four tries before my hands didn't stink anymore and it was safe to go back to the party.

You could see the fireworks from the town park over the trees in Tommy's yard, so we stayed for those and for dessert.

People started to slip away and the grown-ups were cleaning up. Kennedy was half asleep on Dad's lap. Tommy and I sat around talking and laughing—Eddie's mom had already picked him up and Josh had gone home—when the twins came and sat with us.

"Did you do it?" Dante asked.

I nodded.

"Did it work?" Malik asked.

"I think so."

"You should have seen us blasting that slime!" Tommy showed them how he had held the blaster.

As we told them the whole story the twins said

things like, "Woah, dude!" and laughed in all the right places.

I was proud of myself as I made my way home with my family. I almost wished I could tell Mom and Dad how I had been brave and banished the ghosts, but they'd only tell me there was no such thing again.

Dad pushed the front door open and jumped back with a hand over his nose. "It smells like a sewer exploded."

Mom stuck her head in and then pulled it out. "What in the world?"

Dad put Kennedy down and she kind of whimpered for a second, then the smell woke her up, too. "It's stinky."

Even Fillmore, who loves gross smells, didn't want to go inside.

Dread washed over me the same way it did when Mom and Dad had used the words *family meeting* at the beginning of the summer. *I'm in big trouble.*

"Wait here." Dad pulled his shirt up over his mouth and nose and stepped into the house. He went from room to room. He didn't say another word until he got upstairs. "It smells like it's coming from the attic!" he yelled down to us.

I heard him open the door and go up the stairs.

His face was white and grim when he came back.

Are the ghosts back? Did he see one?

Dad had a slime blaster in one hand and a broken, smelly egg in the other. "Roosevelt, what do you know about this?"

CHAPTER THIRTEEN
A Mighty Stink

I stared at the broken egg in Dad's hand. The smell was still so strong that Mom took a step backwards.

"I thought the mighty stink would be gone by the time the party ended," I mumbled. "It was to make the ghosts leave."

"The whole house smells!"

My dad hardly ever yells at anything other than the news on TV, but he said that loud enough to be heard all over the neighborhood. Mom was looking at me with her most serious expression, and Kennedy started to cry.

"Are there more of these?" Dad asked. If he was in a cartoon there would be smoke coming out of his ears or his head would be exploding.

I nodded, pressing my lips together. Dad was starting to be scarier than the ghosts.

"How many?"

"Three," I said.

"Do you know where they are?"

"Sort of," I answered. The truth was that I had thrown them kind of wildly. I'd been surrounded by ghosts and slime blasters at the time.

Dad turned to Mom. "I'm going to set the tent up in the backyard. I don't know how long it will take for the smell to dissipate. And then Roosevelt and I will find the other three eggs and get them out of the house."

It's a good thing the ghosts are gone, I thought, *because I am going to have to go up to the attic in the D-A-R-K.*

"At least all of our camping gear is in the garage," Mom said.

Dad was silent while he carried the tent into the backyard and I kept my mouth shut, too. While he was setting up, I found the sleeping bags and carried them outside.

Kennedy flopped into the grass, already nearly asleep.

"I can't believe I'm going to have to sleep on the ground when I'm this pregnant," Mom said.

"Roosevelt!" Dad barked. "Go up to the deck and get a lounge chair. We'll bring it into the tent for your mom."

"Good idea," Mom said, smiling at him.

I wished I had come up with the idea myself. She watched me make my way toward the deck. Our motion-sensor lights came on, and there it was in plain sight—her potato-salad bowl.

"Roosevelt," she said. "You told me you didn't know where that bowl was."

"I said I couldn't *see* it," I said. "And I couldn't. I wasn't looking at it when you asked."

"And what did you do with it?" she asked.

"I made slime."

"Is that what's all over the floor upstairs?" Dad

asked.

"We blasted the ghosts with it," I answered.

"And what were the rotten eggs for?" he asked.

"Ghosts don't like mighty stinks. They were the mighty stink."

Dad rubbed his face and then quickly pulled his hands away. "Ugh, my hands smell."

"Kennedy's bubbles will help get it off," I said.

Dad sighed. "What else did you do? Slime and stink. What else?"

"We played old-lady opera music really loud. No one likes that. Not even ghosts."

Mom was pressing her lips together like she was trying not to laugh.

Dad stared at me for a minute, and I was afraid he was going to tell me about the history of opera music, but he didn't. He finished the tent and moved the lounge chair inside while I carried the sleeping bags. Kennedy crawled into hers with her Dolley Madison doll and was out in less than a minute.

"Let's go," Dad said to me. "We have to open all the windows in the house and you're going to help me find the rest of those eggs. And after we've done that, and I'm a lot less angry than I am now, you and I will have a talk about this silly idea of yours about ghosts."

"We don't have to talk about them anymore," I said. "I banished them. They went out the window. I saw."

Dad shook his head and huffed really loud. He had been doing a lot of that. "Follow me."

We went through the back door, leaving it open behind us. The windows were mostly closed because of air conditioning so we opened them in every room. I had to admit the stink was a mighty one, and the closer we got to the attic the mightier it got. I was starting to feel a little sick to my stomach from it, but I didn't think I should tell Dad that.

After we opened every single window in the rest of the house, it was time to go to the attic. It was dark, but I reminded myself that the ghosts were gone.

Dad opened the attic door, and the smell hit me in the face. It was even worse than before. Dad turned on the light—still the single bare bulb hanging from the ceiling—and I followed him upstairs.

"Where are they?" He pulled a shopping bag out of his pocket.

I pointed to the far-left corner where one had smashed against the wall and dripped to the floor. Dad was on his way to get it when he slipped on the slime and landed on his butt.

"I'll get it," I said. I grabbed another one that had smashed into the wall on the way back. "There's one more." I looked around. The smell was so bad that I couldn't even follow my nose to find it.

Dad spotted it before me. He threw it into the bag with the others and we rushed outside. Dad dumped them and made sure the trash-can lid was locked in place.

"My hands stink," I said. I didn't say that his did, too.

The two of us went into the half bath downstairs—the one farthest from the attic—and scrubbed our hands lots of times with mom's fancy company soap. Then we dried them on her fancy company towels.

"Bed. Now." Dad turned out the light and I followed him to the tent. Fillmore was already asleep on top of my sleeping bag and I had to curl around him.

"We'll talk about this in the morning," Dad said.

Just before I fell asleep I heard Mom and Dad whispering. Dad had his hand on Mom's beach-ball belly and they were talking about baby Carter and how great she was going to be.

"That's some kick. I hope she's not going to cause any trouble," Dad said.

Mom chuckled. "She'd better not."

"If she does, we'll have to give her back."

Mom laughed again. "It's a deal."

I'm not some little kid. I knew parents couldn't give kids away just because they didn't like them, but I felt like I did when I was in the middle of the attic surrounded by the mighty stink—like I might throw up, cry, or both. I stuck my nose into Fillmore's soft fur, hoping that by morning the smell would be gone.

Do Mom and Dad wish they could give me away?

CHAPTER FOURTEEN
Big Trouble

When I woke up the next morning I was alone in the tent and I could already feel the sun warming up the tent walls. It would be hot in here soon. I peeked out of the flap. Fillmore and Dad were sitting in the shade on the deck. Tendrils of steam, like teeny, tiny ghost babies, rose from Dad's coffee cup.

It hit me all at once, remembering the mighty stink and how angry Dad had been—angrier than I had ever seen him—and how he'd threatened to give baby Carter back if she caused trouble. He still looked mad, but maybe not *as* mad. There was one sure way to get him to cheer up, and I took it.

"Teddy Roosevelt liked to go camping, didn't he?" I asked, ducking through the tent flap. "Wasn't he hiking and camping in Vermont when President McKinley died? Someone had to climb a mountain to find him, right?"

"It was the Adirondacks in New York," Dad said, "not Vermont. And you're not going to get out of this that easily." Dad stared at me for a long minute—something parents did when they wanted you to pay attention, or some junk like that.

"I want you to listen very carefully," Dad said slowly. "There is no such thing as ghosts. The attic is not and never was haunted."

"But—" I was going to tell him we were safe, that I had banished the ghosts, but he didn't let me talk.

"No buts. You are going to spend the day with me in the attic cleaning up your mess. You'd better hope that slime didn't stain the floors or the wall. Any extra money to fix the damage will be coming from your allowance and your birthday and report-card money from Grandma and Grandpa until it's paid for."

I gasped. Allowance was one thing, but my

report-card money? "Did you tell Grandma?" I asked. "She won't like that."

Dad only glared at me.

Darn! Even after paying for the stink bombs, I had enough to buy that model of the Mars Rover. I was hoping Dad and I would build it together.

"C'mon," he said. "The smell is better. Wash up and have some breakfast and then we'll get started."

"Eddie's coming over to—"

"Not today. I called his mom," Dad said.

"Is he in trouble? Are Tommy and Josh?"

"Whose house is this?" Dad asked.

"Ours," I answered.

"Who started all this ghost nonsense?"

I'm supposed to say me here, but really it was the ghosts who started it, I thought. "Me, I guess."

"And who was behind the mess you caused last night?"

Dante and Malik.

Dad wouldn't like that either so I said, "me," again.

"Your friends aren't in trouble," he said with one of those old-people sighs. "Now go and get changed and have some breakfast. We have work to do."

As I was going through the back door, Mom and Kennedy were going out the front. Mom looked tired from sleeping outside with a baby the size of a beach ball in her belly. That baby was going to be super fat, that's for sure.

"Sorry, Mom," I said.

"I know," she answered. "But you still have to clean up your mess. Kennedy and I are spending the day at Aunt Jessica's stink-free house."

I didn't point out that Aunt Jessica's baby made a mighty stink of its own.

"P-U," Kennedy said, plugging her nose. "Roosevelt made it stinky!"

"Sorry," I said again.

"We'll talk later," Mom told me. "You listen to your father today."

I nodded. *It's not like I have a choice.*

Dad sent me across the street to take care of the rabbits after breakfast. "And come right back," he said.

Tommy came out to help. Dante and Malik walked over, too—not to help.

"Why didn't you tell me those eggs would make the whole house smell?" I asked. "I'm in big trouble."

Dante laughed. "But you said the ghosts are gone."

"I bet you're still scared to sleep up there, aren't you?" Malik asked. "You're a big chicken—or a scared little rabbit."

"Am not," I said. "But maybe *you* should be afraid. Those ghosts flew out my window and I think I saw them fly into yours."

"They did not," Malik said.

"I saw a green shimmer fly out of my window and head across the street. I'd be careful if I were you," I said.

"If ghosts are going to bother anyone in my house, it'll be our songbird here," Malik rubbed Tommy's head. "Oh wait, they don't like loud, old-lady music."

"Quit it," Tommy yelled, pushing his hand away.

"Besides, ghosts like to stay in the same place whenever they can. They probably flew right back into your window as soon as they could," Dante added.

I glared at him, but inside I was wondering—*is that true?* "It still stinks," I said. "It's going to stink for a long time."

"Look," Dante teased. "He's scared."

Malik started making chicken noises.

"I am not scared." I tried to come up with some junk that would prove I wasn't. "I'm going to be sleeping outside until my new room is ready—all night—by myself. Would a chicken do that?"

"You spend the night outside by yourself and we'll stop calling you a chicken," Dante said. "But if you don't—"

"But if you don't—" Malik jumped in, "you have to do a cannonball at the town pool flapping your

arms and yelling, 'I'm a chicken! I'm a chicken!'"

"Cannonballs aren't allowed at the town pool," I said. "They'll tell me I can't come back for a month."

Malik grinned. "Better not be a chicken then."

"Do we have a deal?" Dante asked. "Or do we call you a chicken from now on?" He stuck out his hand.

"Deal," I said, shaking on it. "I'm doing it."

Malik turned on his heel and Dante followed him back into the house. "Later, losers," he said over his shoulder.

"Are you really going to sleep out at night by yourself?" Tommy asked.

"I am now," I answered. I swallowed hard. "Can't be a chicken, can I?"

"You banished ghosts," Tommy said. "You're brave. You can be in your backyard by yourself all night. It'll be easy."

I nodded. I didn't feel as sure as Tommy sounded. But I had no other choice.

CHAPTER FIFTEEN

Roosevelt Banks is *Not* a Chicken

Dad and I worked upstairs most of the morning. We put some of Mom's peppermint oil under our noses and wore those construction masks that Dante and Malik made such a big deal about taking off the other day. It helped with the stink, but not with the big, heavy knot in my stomach. Things would be going okay for a while and then I'd remember Dad joking about wanting to give me back.

"The people of Gettysburg, Pennsylvania had to walk around with peppermint oil under their noses for weeks after the big Civil War battle," Dad said.

"Because there were so many ghosts?" I asked.

"No ghosts!"

Questions about history junk usually cheer Dad up. I guess that wasn't the right one.

"They wore peppermint oil because so many animals and people died in the battle. The smell lingered until the first frost," he said.

"A mighty stink?"

He nodded. "A mighty stink."

"Was there a mighty stink when Abraham Lincoln was there?"

"He gave the Gettysburg Address in November— months after the battle ended," Dad answered. He stood in the middle of the room under the creepy, bare light bulb and looked around. "Let's get back to work."

The green slime cleaned up pretty easily, but three of those stink bombs left a slimy, smelly trail on two of the wall boards and on one piece of insulation. Dad said we'd have to put new pieces in.

"Is that expensive?" I asked. I was thinking about my Mars Rover.

I got the Dad-eye. "Worried about your report-card money?"

Caught!

"I just wondered," I said.

"It's not that expensive, but it's still coming out of your pocket," Dad said.

It was kind of nice working side by side with Dad. Not as fun as all the things I had on my SUMMER OF DAD list, but pretty okay. And the good news was that I didn't see or hear anything to make me think that the ghosts had come back. I didn't like that giant, gaping hole where the desk and drawers were going in, but I didn't think ghosts were lurking there.

We had lunch on the back deck and talked like I wasn't in big, huge trouble.

"I think we can sleep inside tonight," Dad said. "Maybe even close the windows and turn on the air conditioning. We'll see what your mom says when she gets home."

"I'm going to sleep in the tent anyway," I said.

"You and your friends, like mountain men?" Dad said.

"No, by myself," I said. "I'm not afraid."

"I didn't say you were afraid. But not *all* by yourself, right? You and Fillmore?" Dad asked.

"No, by myself—no Fillmore," I told him.

"Won't that be scary?" Dad asked.

Yes! Very scary. But I shook my head. Inside I was thinking, *tell me I can't unless you sleep outside with me.* If my parents said no then the twins couldn't call me a chicken.

But Dad didn't say no. "As long as you stay in the backyard. No wandering anywhere."

"No wandering," I said.

Not unless I'm in a bear's stomach. Then I won't be able to help it.

I was half hoping Mom would say she could still smell the stink and the whole family was going to have to sleep outside again, but she didn't. And she didn't tell me I couldn't sleep outside by myself, either.

Why aren't parents strict when you want them to be?

After Kennedy's bedtime I put on my pajamas, brushed my teeth, and got ready to sleep in the tent. I filled a bag with my book about space, a flashlight, my phone—in case I had to call 911 to report being kidnapped by a bear—and some snacks.

"Wait, I shouldn't bring snacks, should I?" I said. "They might attract a bear."

Dad smiled. "You'd be more likely to attract a raccoon or some field mice."

Raccoons? Field mice?

"What do you think, Mom?"

"Have you already brushed your teeth?"

I nodded.

"Leave the snacks then. But bring a bottle of water in case you get thirsty."

"Ooo-kay," I said slowly. I made a big deal out of saying good night and heading toward the back door. I gave them lots of chances to change their minds—not because I was scared, but because it would be a total bummer to get all comfortable in my sleeping bag and then have to turn around and come back inside because Mom got worried or some junk like that.

I knelt in front of Fillmore. "Don't be scared," I told him. "I'm only going to be in the backyard, but you can't come. You can sleep with Mom and Dad tonight."

"Come, Fillmore," Dad called.

Fillmore ran over to him wagging his tail. He didn't even notice when I slid open the back door and slipped outside.

Traitor!

I would be outside on my own for the whole night, and no one could call me a chicken. Except maybe a bear.

CHAPTER SIXTEEN

Roosevelt Banks, Mountain Man

I marched to the tent like a mountain man. I didn't even turn on my flashlight until I opened the flap. Then I checked for raccoons and mice. Even mountain men don't like raccoons jumping all over them while they sleep. All of the sleeping bags were still there. Seeing them all together made me feel a little lonely, but then I remembered—*I'm a mountain man. I am* NOT *a chicken.*

I got into my sleeping bag and started to read about space. Then I felt something weird by my foot. *A spider?* I jumped out and checked inside my bag for what Mom called unwelcome visitors. I didn't see any.

The motion-sensor lights in the yard clicked off and all of a sudden it was much, much darker. And all I had was my flashlight.

There was a little squeak and I started to think about field mice. I saw one in the shed once, with the lawn mower and the rake and the big bag of dirt Mom used for plants. A tent was a way nicer place to live than a big bag of dirt. *What if it—*

I jumped up again. This time I got on top of Mom's lawn chair with my sleeping bag. *Mice can't climb lawn chairs, can they?*

Kennedy's Dolley Madison doll was poking out of the top of her princess sleeping bag. Maybe in the dark Dolley would look like something field mice and raccoons don't want to mess with. I stood her up right in front of the tent flap and turned off my flashlight. In the dark, she might look pretty tough to a raccoon or a mouse.

I got back into my sleeping bag for the third time. *Did a spider or a mouse get into my bed when I was setting*

Dolley up as a guard?

I checked again—every nook and cranny, every seam—and decided it was safe. I lay back with my book about space and took a deep breath. *I am a mountain man,* I told myself, *sleeping outside by myself because I'm not scared. Not one bit.*

The next thing I knew, I was waking up in the pitch dark. I reached around wildly for my book and my flashlight and found them on the tent floor. I turned the flashlight on and nothing happened. I tried again and again. The batteries were dead!

I was alone in the middle of the night and I had no light. No way to see what was coming at me. My heart pounded so hard I thought it would burst right out of my chest. And then I saw it—something right by the tent flap. Something raccoon-sized, ready to give me rabies.

I waved my arms, but it didn't move. It just sat there, staring. Getting ready to take a big bite out of me. I waved my arms even bigger and I hit it! It fell right over like a—*like a doll.*

"That's Dolley Madison," I said out loud. "Not a crazy, hungry raccoon."

I sat back, relieved. "Dolley Madison," I said again.

So I didn't have a hungry raccoon after me—not yet, anyway—but I *did* have the problem of the broken flashlight. I was either going to have to walk through the backyard by myself in the middle of the night or spend the whole night in the dark.

Which one is scarier?

I decided that if a wild animal was going to come at me in the middle of the night, then I should be able to see it. Mountain men fought off things like bears and mountain lions and zombie raccoons all the time. They had to have light to do that.

I moved Dolley aside. I felt silly, but I told her I'd be right back. If anything was out there lurking, I wanted it to believe I wasn't alone. "Keep guarding the tent," I said in the deepest, scratchiest voice I could make.

I opened the zipper on the tent flap and stuck my head out. There were about thirty feet between me and the steps to the deck and the sliding-glass door into the house.

What if Mom and Dad forgot I'm out here and locked the door?

I had no choice. I had to make a run for and it and hope the door was unlocked.

I turned my head from side to side, making sure nothing was waiting to eat me.

Nothing so far.

I stuck my body halfway out and did it again. I froze. There was something in the corner of the yard. Something big. Something as black as night. Something like—*a bear!*

Did it move?

Did it growl?

I slipped back inside the tent and zipped the zipper. My heart was pounding again and something was doing jumping jacks in my stomach.

Did a mouse crawl down my throat while I was sleeping? Was it jumping around in my stomach trying to get out? Gross!

I shook my head. I couldn't worry about mice now—not when there was a bear, ready and waiting to claw me to death. A tent zipper was no match for a bear's sharp claws and teeth. I had to get to safety.

I stood up, unzipped that zipper, and took off. I ran as fast as I could to the deck. The motion-sensor lights came on and I stumbled up the steps in the sudden glare. The bear was on my heels.

I eyed the door. *Please don't be locked.*

The bear's breath was hot on my neck. *Please don't be locked.*

I smelled whatever was left of the rotten meat from the creature's last meal. *Please don't be locked.*

I heard its paws pounding on the deck behind me. *Please don't be locked.*

I felt a claw grabbing at my pajama top, reaching

for skin. *Please don't be locked.*

I got to the door. *Not locked!* I slammed it open, dashed inside, and then locked it behind me before I slumped to the floor

Dad was sitting in his favorite chair, reading.

He looked up. "Everything okay, Roosevelt?"

"B... B... B... Bear!"

Dad stood next to me by the sliding-glass door. "Where?" he asked.

"It chased me," I said, trying to catch my breath.

"Are you sure? I don't see anything."

How can Dad be so calm when I nearly died?

"I saw it there, in the corner of the yard, and when I ran for the house it chased me," I said.

That's when I looked—really looked—in the corner of the yard with all the lights on. It wasn't a bear. It was one of Mr. Fredericks'—our neighbor's—bushes.

"Not a bear," I said. "But I think a mouse crawled down my throat while I was sleeping. It's jumping around in my stomach."

"A mouse couldn't crawl down your throat." Dad put his arm around my shoulders. "I think sleeping outside by yourself will have to wait a couple of years," he said. "How about if I stay out there with you, just for tonight?"

"You can't," I said. "It was a dare. If I don't sleep outside by myself then I'm going to have to tell everyone at the pool I'm a chicken and flap my arms like one, too."

"What?"

"Dante and Malik—they dared me to sleep outside by myself. They're going to come and check in the morning," I explained.

"Sleep outside by yourself, or without another human?"

"What do you mean?" I asked.

"How about Fillmore?" Dad asked. "He's been wandering around, not knowing what to do with himself without you in your bed."

"I don't know. I shook on it."

"How about this—you spend the night outside with Fillmore and I'll come and get him early in the morning, before the twins come over to check," Dad said.

I thought about it.

"Technically, you're still doing the dare," Dad said. "Nothing chicken about that."

"You sure?" I asked.

"I'm sure," he said.

Fillmore in tow and new batteries in my flashlight, Dad walked me to the tent.

"Hey, how come you're still awake?" I asked. "It's the middle of the night."

"It's not that late. You must have only slept for a little while." He climbed into the tent with me and smiled when he saw the doll standing guard. "Dolley Madison protected the White House when the British marched into Washington during the War of 1812," he said.

I snuggled into my sleeping bag, Fillmore at my feet. "I know," I said with a yawn. "She saved the picture of George…"

I was asleep before I finished the sentence.

CHAPTER SEVENTEEN
Who's the Chicken Now?

The next morning Dad came outside super early to get Fillmore. It was already light, so I didn't mind. I put Dolley back inside Kennedy's sleeping bag and lay down. I wanted it to look like I was asleep when Dante and Malik came to check on me.

It took forever for them to show up.

Finally, I heard them laughing and trying to be quiet when they entered the backyard. They were planning to scare me somehow. But it was time to turn the tables on them.

They unzipped the tent, slowly and quietly. Just when they were about to throw the flap open and do whatever they were going to do, I leapt out at them and growled like a hungry bear.

Malik screamed and Dante fell on his butt trying to scramble away. The water balloons Malik carried were broken on the ground. I grabbed Dante's balloons quickly and threw them both at the twins.

Nailed them!

I cracked up while the twins wiped water from their eyes.

"Who's chicken now?" I asked.

"Not so fast," Dante said. "We have to check that tent."

Malik ran over and stuck his head inside. "There are four sleeping bags in there," he said. "Aww… is that princess bag yours?"

"That sleeping bag is Kennedy's, and they're all still in there from the Fourth of July. My whole family slept outside because of the mighty stink. I slept in the tent by myself last night. Ask my dad."

Kennedy ran outside then, wanting to go and see the bunnies before she had to leave for daycare with

Mom. Fillmore was on her heels.

"Ask her," Dante said. "She'll tell the truth."

Thank goodness Kennedy was asleep when I went inside the house last night.

"Hey, Kennedy," Malik said. "Did your brother sleep outside by himself last night?"

"Roosevelt slept in the tent," she said.

"Where was the dog?" Dante asked.

Kennedy started to giggle. "Fillmore slept in my bed. He licked my face to wake me up."

Good old Fillmore!

"You sure?" Dante asked.

"Yes. He woke me up." She turned to me. "Roosevelt, I want to go see the bunnies."

"Okay, okay," I said. "Let me get dressed, then I'll take you."

As I made my way past the twins I couldn't help but let out some chicken noises. "Bye, chickens," I said. "See you later. Try not to scream when you see me coming."

I was still chuckling when I walked upstairs to my room.

I didn't see the twins again until that afternoon. I was hanging out with Tommy in his bedroom after play rehearsal when the twins pounded down the stairs, laughing at something or other and shouting the word, "Revenge!"

"What are they up to?" I asked Tommy.

He shrugged. "They've been holed up there since I got home. Some kind of secret project. It's probably better not to know."

I wondered if *Revenge* had something to do with me.

I texted Josh to see if he had heard anything at baseball camp. I waited a few minutes for him to text back.

Whispers. Yr name
Will try 2 find out more.

I showed it to Tommy.

"I'll try, too," he said. "The last thing you want is to be on the other end of one of their dirty tricks."

CHAPTER EIGHTEEN
Moving Day

Days passed and I forgot all about the twins and their revenge. They helped Mr. Williams and Dad in the attic once and were there when the carpenter came to build the drawers and the desk. Dad surprised me with a desk chair on wheels that spins around, which was cool.

Mom let me choose the paint color—blue—and I helped Dad paint the walls. Mom bought a rug and matching bedspreads for the two beds, and the creepy bare light bulb was replaced with what looked like a spaceship. We were only waiting for the new mattresses to be delivered.

Dad and I carried most of my things upstairs. Sunday night was going to be my first night in my new room. Tommy was sleeping over, along with Josh and Eddie.

Dad was sitting on one of the beds with a notebook in his hand when I got upstairs with a pile of clothes.

"THE SUMMER OF DAD," he said.

"Yeah, I thought…"

"You thought we were going to be able to hang out for the whole summer."

I nodded.

Dad ran a finger down the list. "You had a lot of fun things planned."

I nodded again.

"I guess this summer has been pretty disappointing so far," he said.

Yeah, this new baby ruined everything.

I could see he felt bad, so I pretended the summer wasn't ruined. "I built a fort with the guys and slept outside like a mountain man and junk like that." I was about to mention Operation Banish Ghosts, which was the coolest thing ever, but I remembered how mad he had been about that, so I kept my mouth shut.

"Tell you what. We can still do some of these things before the end of the summer. How about we go on a campout at the state park this weekend? We can ask Tommy to come."

"He's in *The Sound of Music*," I said. "Mom already bought tickets for all of us for Saturday night. And on Sunday Tommy's coming for a barbecue and then a sleepover in my new room. Eddie and Josh, too. Mom said we could."

"Okay then," Dad said. "We'll do something Saturday afternoon just the two of us."

"A history thing?" I asked. You had to be careful about that stuff with my dad.

"Fishing, maybe, or a baseball game. I'll check if the team's playing a home game," he said. "Hey, you're not still afraid of ghosts, are you? Is that why you want your friends here that first night?"

I wanted to tell him that I had banished the ghosts but then he'd start going on again about how there was no such thing. "No ghosts," I said. "I just thought it would be fun."

Dad kept his word. On Saturday we went fishing, and he promised me I wouldn't have to eat any of the fish. I caught three and he only caught two and we threw them all back, but the whole time we were fishing we were talking and laughing and having a great time.

That night Mom made us all dress nice for opening night of *The Sound of Music*. Kennedy put on all of her sparkly jewelry and her fanciest dress, but the rest of us looked like normal people. We snagged seats right in the front row, next to Tommy's parents and brothers.

"First night in your new room tomorrow?" Dante asked.

"Yup. The guys are sleeping over."

Malik started to laugh and Dante nudged him with an elbow.

"Sure those ghosts are all gone?" Dante asked.

I glared at him. I wasn't going to let him scare me. "GONE," I said loudly, which made everyone look at me and one old lady say "shush."

The play hadn't even started yet, but Mr. Williams

made the twins move so that they were between their parents and couldn't bother anyone normal.

And then the play started and I forgot all about the twins and the ghosts and my new room. It was a pretty girly show about love and junk, but Tommy was great in it—singing and dancing and even being funny. The whole audience laughed at one of his lines and I sat up a little straighter thinking, *that's my friend*.

After, we all went to the cast party backstage and then both families went out for ice cream, even though it was late and Kennedy looked all droopy.

Dante and Malik made chicken noises at Tommy and me whenever our parents were busy doing other things, and they kept laughing. What that was about I don't know. But it definitely had something to do with me and my new room.

CHAPTER NINETEEN
Brave for Real

Sunday morning Eddie came over early to help with the rabbits. Josh didn't have baseball camp, and Tommy had Sunday and Monday off from the play. It was our first time all hanging out together in ages. After our sleepover, Dad said he'd take all of us to the lake at the state park for the day on Monday. It was going to be EPIC!

Mrs. C. came outside to tell us that it was almost time to get the new baby bunnies neutered so that she could find new homes for them. She already had takers for Armstrong and Aldrin.

"What about Flopsy?" I asked.

Mrs. C. smiled. "She's mine for life. I think I'm going to move her into the house with me. Once the others are adopted. I don't want her to be lonely."

Kennedy's eyes got wide. She grabbed my hand and started dragging me toward the street.

"It's Sunday. There's no daycare today," I told her.

"I have to go home NOW!" she announced.

I walked her toward our yard and she took off into the house.

A few minutes later, she stood at the edge of our yard yelling for me to come and get her again. I had my hands full of rabbit-pooped-in hay, so Josh went.

She skipped over and did a little twirl. "I can have *two* bunnies, but not six." She checked out all the bunnies. "That one and that one," she said, pointing. "Or maybe that one and that one. I want them all!"

I thought about who was going to have to take care of them—that would be me. But then I realized how hard Kennedy would be to live with if all the bunnies were adopted by other families, and I felt relieved.

"Go and tell Mrs. C.," I said. "She'll be happy."

Eddie sat at the edge of the hutch. "Maybe my parents will let me take two," he said. "Kennedy can bring their brother and sister over for playdates."

"I'd take two, but Dante and Malik were talking about making little parachutes for them to see if they could skydive from our roof."

Josh laughed. "That would be cool to see."

"Not for the bunnies," I said.

"Yeah, I guess."

Saying the twins' names out loud must have been a kind of curse—they came outside to be obnoxious. They were looking at us and giggling.

They had some kind of plan—something to do with me and ghosts. I had to figure it out before tonight. I was tired of being afraid. I was tired of pretending to be brave.

Tonight I wanted to be brave for real.

Eddie, Josh, and I were hanging out at the fort that afternoon, drinking soda and burping.

Tommy joined us when his family got back from church and lunch at his grandma's. "I know what the twins have planned," he said. "I overheard them. And we're the ones that gave them the idea."

"What idea?" I asked.

"They recorded something on one of their phones—ghost noises. They told your mom they forgot something in the attic and hid a Bluetooth speaker somewhere in your new room. They were talking about how we're going to run out into the street screaming and crying in the middle of the night—and they're going to get it all on video.

'That's actually a pretty cool idea," Eddie said, "if you know not to be scared."

"But we would have been," I said. "Really scared."

"But now they'll do it and we won't be scared at all—the joke's on them," Josh said.

I thought about that for a minute. That would be cool—them waiting around for something big to happen and for it to be a total dud. But then I thought of something that would be even cooler.

"What if they're the ones who are scared? What if they're the ones who run outside screaming in the middle of the night?"

"How are we going to do that?" Eddie asked.

"Let's find that speaker," I said. "Or hide my mom's in your house. We can make our own scary recording."

"There's sound-effects stuff at the community playhouse," Tommy said. "And I know how to use it."

"We can ride our bikes there without permission," I said. "It's included in the list of places we're allowed to go."

Fifteen minutes later Tommy "borrowed" his mom's theater key and we biked there. It was a little weird being backstage with sets and costumes and stuff, but Tommy led us into the sound booth.

"Mr. Casey's the sound guy," Tommy said. "He was showing me how it all works."

We started to play around with sound effects, and they were *amazing*! We started with some loud, heavy footsteps. Then we picked up some big chains and started to shake them before adding rattling bones. There was actually a button for the sound of a door

opening, followed by a slam. Then we made the chains and the rattling bones even louder and added more footsteps.

"Too bad we can't rig the door to open by itself," I said. "That would really scare the pants off them."

Tommy thought about that for a minute. "We could, but it would take too long and they'd probably catch us. Let's just stick with sound effects."

We added loud breathing followed by some ghostly moans. We made the moans louder and louder and added a high-pitched scream, like someone was being murdered.

We all yelled, "I want revenge!" at the same time at the top of our lungs and finished it off with another scream.

We listened to the whole thing and it was AWESOME! I couldn't wait for tonight.

"Where should we hide the speaker?" I asked.

Tommy shrugged. "Their room is such a mess they won't notice one more thing on their bookshelf.

We can hide it there."

"How can we make sure they're in their room when we play the recording?" Eddie asked.

"We'll wait until after they play the recording they made for us," I said. "They'll be super disappointed that we're not running around screaming. And then we'll nail them!"

The four of us high fived.

"Who's getting revenge now?" I asked.

"Operation Banish Brothers," Tommy said with a laugh.

CHAPTER TWENTY
Operation Banish Brothers

It was really hard to wait to enact our plan. I wanted to see Dante and Malik freak out *now*. Slipping the speaker into their bedroom was easy, but we had to wait until nighttime and quiet to banish them and their teasing.

We had a barbecue on my back deck complete with s'mores while Dad and Kennedy talked about names for her new bunnies. Dad wanted to name them after first ladies. Kennedy wanted names like Princess Buttercup and Princess Snowdrop. I remembered how Kennedy had stood up to Dante and Malik when they were trying to pester the bunnies and I knew she would win. Dad was no match for Kennedy.

After we had our fill of s'mores, the guys and I went up to THE ATTIC OF DUDES to hang out. We took turns spinning in the desk chair and wheeling it across the room. Dad had set up a TV in my room—for one night only. We told him we were having a Harry Potter movie marathon but really we were just waiting until we could exact our revenge on Dante and Malik.

Finding the speaker they had planted was super easy. It was in a desk drawer, which they had left partly open.

At 9 o'clock we played rock, paper, scissors to see who was going to have to sleep in the sleeping bags instead of the beds. Then we turned the lights out and pretended to go to sleep.

"It won't take long," Tommy said quietly. "They're super impatient."

He was right. A few minutes later we heard them giggling under my window. Then Dante told Malik to "turn it on already." And Malik told Dante to have his phone ready to make a video.

Josh's eyes lit up. "We have to take a video of them when we scare them!"

I gave him a thumbs up. We didn't want the twins to hear us.

"Your brothers better not become robbers," I whispered. "They'd be caught in a flash."

"Or zombie hunters," Eddie said with a chuckle.

"Good, then they'd be in jail—or eaten by zombies," Tommy whispered back.

A second later, the recording started. We had turned the speaker way down low, but we could still hear it. Compared to ours, their ghost noises were totally lame. Our recording was way better.

We lay still, keeping the lights off, while the twins slowly realized that their plan hadn't worked.

Ha!

Then they started arguing about which one of them had screwed up. I peeked out the window and watched them walk across the street.

Eddie reached to turn the light on and I stopped him. "If they see the light, they'll know we're awake," I said.

It was getting to be hard to stay awake with all the quiet. I turned my flashlight on and started to read out loud from *Hatchet*. I had to admit that Mr. Casey had been right—it was a really good book.

Tommy kept his eyes on his house across the street. We waited and waited. Finally the twins' light went out and we waited just a little bit more.

I told Mom and Dad that we had to get something from Tommy's room.

"Come right back," Mom said. "I don't like you wandering around in the dark."

Dad stood up. "I'll watch them from the front door."

I frowned. Dad watching wasn't part of the plan, but there wasn't anything we could do about it. We crossed the street and went around to Tommy's back door. Eddie, Josh, and I stood in the shadows on the side of the house while Tommy went inside carrying his phone and a speaker the twins had planted in my room.

He must have told his parents the same thing as mine—right before he placed the second speaker outside the twins' bedroom door. They were going to hear the scary ghost noises from TWO different speakers. They wouldn't know which way to run.

The rest of us had our phone cameras ready to make videos.

It only took a minute. We heard screams and a clatter of loud footsteps pounding down the stairs and through the house. Dante and Malik tore out of the back door so fast that they stumbled into the yard holding onto each other.

Tommy was right behind them, grinning. He held up his phone. "Smile for the camera!"

"No!" I shouted. "Look this way. We'll make you movie stars!"

The twins stood there, holding each other up, more shocked than they had ever been in their lives.

Mr. and Mrs. Williams were confused, but Tommy, Eddie, Josh, and I were cracking up and high fiving each other.

"Operation Banish Brothers!" Tommy shouted.

"Do we want to know what just happened?" Mr. Williams asked us.

Tommy and I were laughing too hard to answer.

"Probably not," Josh said. "But Dante and Malik know not to be jerks to us anymore."

I waggled my phone. "Or we'll show the whole middle school what chickens they really are."

Tommy held his phone up, too. "And we've got it from every angle."

My dudes and I cracked up again. Operation Banish Brothers was a victory.

Dad was still standing at the door when we got back to my house.

"Everything okay?" he asked. "I thought I heard

yelling."

"Everything's great!" I said. "C'mon guys, let's go hang out in my new ghost- and twin-free room."

THE SUMMER OF GHOSTS had turned into THE SUMMER OF BRAVE.

CHAPTER TWENTY-ONE

The Attic of Dudes

By the time summer ended and school started, a lot had changed. My room became the official hangout—THE ATTIC OF DUDES—and we had lots of fun up there.

Dad and I did a bunch of cool things—sometimes on our own, sometimes with my friends, and sometimes with Mom and Kennedy. One fun thing we did by ourselves was a camping trip to Gettysburg, Pennsylvania—the place of the original mighty stink from the Civil War. There were signs about ghost tours all over town and I talked Dad into taking one with me, but it was kind of lame. I was starting to believe he was right about there not being any such thing as ghosts.

We had to cut our trip a day short because baby Carter decided to come five weeks early. We rushed home and Dad got there in time to see her get born while Grandma and Grandpa watched me and Kennedy. Carter Julie Banks was in an incubator for a couple of weeks, but then she came home.

Her face was all scrunched up at first and she cried a lot, but she really wasn't so bad when her diaper wasn't giving off a mighty stink and she wasn't barfing all over the place. She liked to grab onto my finger with her little hand and that was kind of cute.

Kennedy was crazy in love with her—so much that she kind of forgot about her bunnies and I had to take care of them. I would have complained, but one day I overheard her and Dad telling Carter what a great big brother I was, and I forgave her.

Dad started sleeping in my extra bed whenever Carter cried too much, and let me tell you—if you think bears are loud, you should hear my dad snore!

I finally had to tell him, "Dad—baby cries are nothing to be afraid of. You have to sleep in your own room."

It might not have been THE SUMMER OF DAD that I expected. But it did turn out to be THE SUMMER OF THE BIG BROTHER.

Laurie Calkhoven had her own attic bedroom growing up complete with a built-in desk and a chair on wheels that spun around and there were definitely no ghosts. After writing ROOSEVELT BANKS, GOOD-KID-IN-TRAINING she missed her main character and his band of bike-dudes-in-training, so she dreamed up this new adventure for them. She lives and works in New York City and is the author of many books for young readers.

Debbie Palen is an illustrator whose work has found a home in children's and middle grade publishing. Currently she resides in Cleveland, Ohio in a house that she hopes isn't haunted, with one human and a very fuzzy animal that might be a cat. When not illustrating, she enjoys walking in the woods and playing her theremin.

Clifton Park-Halfmoon Library

0000605683556